Anonymous

The Highland Monthly

Volume 5

Anonymous

The Highland Monthly
Volume 5

ISBN/EAN: 9783337160173

Printed in Europe, USA, Canada, Australia, Japan

Cover: Foto ©Andreas Hilbeck / pixelio.de

More available books at **www.hansebooks.com**

No. 49.   APRIL 1893.   VOL. V.

THE

HIGHLAND

MONTHLY

CONTENTS.

"NORTHERN CHRONICLE" OFFICE, INVERNESS.

EDINBURGH:
JOHN MENZIES & CO.; OLIVER & BOYD; JAMES THIN.

Glasgow: JOHN MENZIES & CO., and W. & R. HOLMES.

Oban: THOMAS BOYD.

PRICE SIXPENCE.

CONTENTS

The Highland Monthly.

EDITED BY

DUNCAN CAMPBELL, Editor, "Northern Chronicle,"

AND

ALEXANDER MACBAIN, M.A., F.S.A.Scot.

No. 49.   APRIL, 1893.   Vol. V.

FEAR A' GHLINNE.

CAIB. IV.

GHABH Mac 'ic Alasdair a h-uile cothrom air fiosrach-adh fhaotainn mu gach ni a bhuineadh do shuid-heachadh an t-sluaigh, eadar bhochd is bheairteach.   Bha e anabarrach toileach air fios fhaotainn cia mar a bha Fear a' Ghlinne a' riaghladh na h-oighreachd.   Ach ghabh daoine beachd sonraichte air cho tric 'sa bha e a' geur-thiosrachadh mu thimchioll an uachdarain a bh' air a' Ghleann corr is da fhichead bliadhna roimh an am ud. Bha cuid ag radh gu robh a' chuis coltach gur e an ni a bha 'na bheachd an oighreachd a cheannach o Fhear a' Ghlinne, o nach robh duine de'n treibh a bhuineadh do theaghlach a' Ghlinne beo.   Bha cuid eile a' cumail a mach gu robh a' bheag no' mhor de chairdeas aige ri teaghlach a' Ghlinne, on a b'e an aon chinneadh a bh' aigesan agus aig Fear a' Ghlinne.   Agus bha moran de'n t-sluagh bu bheachdaidhe na che le ag radh gu robh e anabarrach coltach 'na chruth 's na chumadh, agus eadhon 'na chainnt, ri Sir Seumas Mor Mac 'ic Alasdair, a bha iomadh bliadhna roimhe sid 'na uachdaran air a' Ghleann.   Tha e coltach nach robh a' bheag anns an rioghachd ri' latha 's ri' linn a bha cho treun

1

ri Sir Seumas, no a thigeadh suas ris anns na h-uile doigh
air an gabhtadh e.　Chaidh e do'n arm an uair a bha e gle
og, agus an am cogadh na h-Eiphit dhearbh e gu'm b'fhior
shaighdear treun e.　Fhuair e o'n Righ tiodal Ridire aig a'
cheart am anns an d'rinneadh Coirneal dheth.　Bha gu
leor de dhaoine beo aig an robh beachd sonraichte air a
chruth agus air a choltas, agus o'n a bha iad a' faicinn ni
eiginn anns an duine uasal a bha' fuireach anns an Taigh
Bhan a bha' cur Shir Seumas 'nan cuimhne, bha iad 'gan
deanamh fhein cinnteach gu robh cairdeas fala agus feola
aca ri' cheile.

An uair a bha muinntir a' Ghlinne mar so a' bruidhinn
am measg a cheile, bha Mac 'ic Alasdair a'dol gu math tric
fo 'smaointean feuch ciod an doigh a b'fhearr anns am
faigheadh e eachdraidh teaghlach a' Ghlinne air chor 's
nach gabhadh neach sam bith amharus gu robh toil aige an
eachdraidh so fhaotainn.　Latha dhe na laithean an uair a
bha e fhein agus Callum Ruadh agus Domhull Sgoileir a'
gabhail cuairt rathad ceann shuas a' Ghlinne, thuirt e,
" Bhuail e anns an inntinn agam o chionn latha no dha
gu'm bu mhath an cur seachad uine dhuinn, gu h-araidh
dhomh fhein, o'n a tha mi 'nam choigreach 'san aite, feasgar
an drasta 'sa rithist a chaitheamh le bhith 'g innseadh
naigheachdan dha cheile mu na nithean a chunnaic agus a
chuala sinn o laithean ar n-oige.　Is iomadh ni a chunnaic
mi fhein, agus is iomadh cunnart troimh 'n deachaidh mi
o'n a thainig cuimhne ugam, ged nach 'eil mi ach og an
coimeas ribhse, fheara, tha mi a' lan-chreidsinn gu'n deachaidh mi troimh chunnartan agus troimh ghabhaidhean a
chuireadh ioghnadh oirbh le cheile."

" Ma ta," arsa Callum Ruadh 's e freagairt, " tha mi
anabarrach deonach a dhol ann an comaidh ruibh fhein
agus ri Domhull Sgoileir mu na h-ursgeulan a chuala sibh
agus mu na driodartan troimh an deachaidh sibh, agus ma
shaoileas sibh gur fhiach mo naigheachdan-sa an eisdeachd,
ni mi mo dhichioll air an aithris dhuibh cho math 's a theid
agam air.　Ach cha mhor is fhiach na th' agamsa de

naigheachdan an coimeas ris na bheil aig Domhull Sgoileir.
Tha mi 'n dochas gu'n aontaich thu, a Dhomhuill, leis an ni
a tha 'nar beachd, agus gu'n toir thu dhuinn sgeula no dha
dhe na chuala tu aig Donnachadh Ban agus aig Mairearad,
a nighean."

" Bheir mise dhuibh, fheara, a h-uile sgeulachd agus
naigheachd a th' air chuimhne agam, agus a shaoileas mi a
chordas ribh. Ach tha eagal orm, a Challuim, gu'n cuala
tu..a a' chuid a' s mo dhiubh roimhe so. Am bheil cuimhne
agad air a liuthad naigheachd agus sgeulachd a dh' aithris
mi dhut fhein agus do Fhear an Rudha a' bhliadhan an
deigh dhut tighinn do'n Taigh Bhan?" arsa Domhull
Sgoileir.

"'S ann agam a tha, agus bidh mi gle thoileach an
cluinntinn a rithist, facal air an fhacal. Mar a tha 'n sean-
fhacal ag radh, Cha mhisde sgeula math innseadh da uair.
Agus ged a chuala mise cuid dhiubh roimhe, cha chuala ar
caraid a h-aon dhiubh riamh roimhe," arsa Callum Ruadh.

" Tha mi ro thoilichte gu bheil sibh le cheile cho deonach
air sgeulachdan agus naigheachdan aithris dhomh. Bha
mi riamh an geall air a bhith 'cluinntinn ursgeulan agus
naigheachdan, agus o nach 'eil moran eile aig fear seach
fear dhinn ri dheanamh air na feasgair fhuara so, tha e cho
math dhuinn a bhith 'gabhail agus ag cisdeachd sgeulachdan ri bhith 'nar tamh,' arsa Mac 'ic Alasdair.

" Is tusa a dh' fheumas toiseachadh an toiseach, a
Dhomhuill," arsa Callum Ruadh.

" Cha 'n ann mar sin a bhios a' chuis idir, a Challuim.
Cuimhnich air an t-sean-fhacal a tha 'g radh, ' A cheud
sgeul air fear an taighe 's gach sgeul gu latha air an aoidh.'
Cha 'n fhaod sinn bristeadh air na seann riaghailtean a bh'
aig na daoine coire o 'n d' thainig sinn. Thug mise dhuibh
sgeulachd bheag an latha bha sinn aig Creag Bhearnaig,
agus cha bhiodh e idir ceart no cothromach toirt orm a'
cheud naigheachd innseadh. Toisich thusa an toiseach
agus an uair a bheir thu dhuinn do naigheachd fhein, no,
sgeul sam bith eile a bhios taitneach, bheir mise dhuibh

sgeul beag no dha mu na sithichean, agus mu shluagh Fhionnlaidh ; ar neo bheir ar deadh charaid dhuinn beachd-sgeul air cuid dhe na nithean a chunnaic agus a chual' e anns na rioghachdan thall," arsa Domhull sgoileir.

Dh' aontaich Callum Ruadh leis na thuirt Domhull Sgoileir, agus shuidhich iad gu'n toisicheadh iad air aithris an cuid naigheachd agus sgeulachd an ath oidhche.

An uair a thainig am feasgar an ath oidhche agus a choinnich na fir anns an t-seomar ur, thoisich Callum Ruadh air innseadh na h-eachdraidh a leanas :—

" Rugadh mise anns an Eilean-Tarsuinn. Bha m' athair aig an am 'na bhuachaille-cruidh aig Domhull an Eilean, mar a theirteadh gu cumanta ris an duine uasal— agus b' esan sin smior an duine uasail—a bha 'na thuath-anach anns an Eilean-Tarsuinn aig an am ud. Bha m' athair air a dhoigh gle mhath ; oir bha carbsa mhor aig Domhull an Eilean ann ; agus mar sin, bha cead aige air crodh is caoraich a chumail dha fhein a bharrachd air na bh' aige fo ainmeachadh tuarasdail. An uair a rachadh Domhull an Eilean gu tir-mor air cheann-gnothaich sam bith, dh' iarradh e air m' athair suil a bhith aige air gach ni a bhuineadh do 'n bhaile. An uair a rachadh e gu margadh a reic no a cheannch chruidh is chaorach, bhiodh m' athair an comhnuidh 'na chuideachd ; agus chuireadh e a chomh-airle ri m' athair an am a bhith 'reic agus a' ceannach. Tha cuimhne gle mhath agamsa air. B'ainneamh aite anns an robh duine cho eireachdail ris. Bha e cho direach air a chnamhan ri mac mathar a sheas am broig leathair. O bhonn gu bathais cha robh meang air. Cha do phos e riamh ; oir bha cumhnanta posaidh eadar e fhein agus nighean Fir-Stocaidh, agus o nach leigeadh a h-athair leatha esan a phosadh, 's e bh' ann cha do phos a h-aon aca riamh.

Bha meas mor aig Domhull an Eilean ormsa. Ged a bha seachdnar de theaghlach aig m' athair 's aig mo mhathair, cha do rainig aois de 'n t-seachdnar ach mise agus Mairi mo phiuthar. Tha e furasda gu leor a thuigsinn

gu robh mi 'faotainn tuilleadh 's a' choir de m' thoil fhein.
Bha eagal air iomadh neach dhe mo luchd-colais nach
tigeadh buaidh no piseach orm am feasd. Bu tric a chuala
mi an sean-fhacal :—

> " Aon mhacan na truaighe,
> 'S dualach gu'n teid e dholaidh."

Mar a bha 'm fortan an dan dhomhsa, ghabh Domhull
an Eilean ceann orm, agus thug e air m' athair mo chur
do 'n sgoil gu ruige Stocaidh. Aig an am ud b' ainneamh
fear no te anns a' chuid de 'n duthaich air an robh mise
eolach, do 'm b' aithne sgriobhadh is leughadh a dheanamh.
Cha deanadh m' athair no mo mhathair a' bheag a
sgriobhadh, mur a rachadh aca air an ainm a sgriobhadh
air eiginn. Ach bha cuid mhath de Bheurla-chluaise aig
m' athair, o'n a bhiodh e gu math tric air tir-mor aig
maragaidhean chruidh is chaorach.

Fhad 's a bha mi 'san sgoil ann an Stocaidh, bha mi
'fuireach ann an taigh a' mhaighstir-sgoile. Is math a tha
cuimhne agam air an latha 'dh' fhalbh m' athair leam gus
m' fhagail air curam a' mhaighstir-sgoile. Cha robh an
t-astar fada; oir cha robh an caolas a bha eadar an
t-Eilean-Tarsuinn agus Stocaidh ach goirid. An uair a
rainig sinn an taigh-sgoile dh' innis m' athair do 'n
mhaighstir-sgoile 'na mo lathair-sa gu robh mi buailteach
air a bhith 'g iarraidh tuilleadh 's a' choir dhe mo thoil
fhein. Dh' earb e ris a' mhaighstir-sgoile mo chumail fo
smachd, agus gun e leigeil leam a bhith bristeadh na
Sabaid. Cha d' iarr e air a theagasg dhomh ach sgriobhadh
is leughadh is cunntas, agus eolas air facal Dhe.

Thainig mi air aghart gle mhath anns an sgoil. Bha
am maighstir-sgoile a' gabhail moran a bharrachd saoith-
reach rium na bha e 'gabhail ris a' chuid eile dhe na
sgoileirean. Bha e air a dheagh phaigheadh air son a
shaoithreach; agus o'n a thainig mi air astar do 'n sgoil,
bha car de mhoit air, gu h-araidh o'n a thuair e litir o
Dhomhull an Eilean ag iarraidh air a bhith gu math
dhomh, agus gu faigheadh e suim airgid uaithe.

Bha mi mu sheachd bliadhna dh' aois 'san am an do chuireadh do 'n sgoil mi, agus bha mi mu thri bliadhna innte. Mu dheireadh dh' fhas mi sgith dhe'n sgoil 's dhe 'n mhaighstir-sgoile. Air ghaol a bhith fior mhath dhomh, bha e 'gam chumail tuilleadh is teann fo smachd. Nan rachainn fad mo choise o'n taigh, dh' fheumainn innseadh c'aite an robh mi. Bhiodh piuthar a' mhaighstir-sgoile a' gabhail mo leith-sgeil cho math 's a dh' fhaodadh i ; ach mar bu trice, dh' fheumadh i a beul a chumail samhach. Ged a bha am maighstir-sgoile 'na dhuine coir, reumail, bha leumannan de 'n chaise ann iomadach uair. Aig an am ud bha mise 'lan chreidsinn gu robh e 'na dhuine cho cas 's a bha beo. Ach tha mi ag aideachadh gu saor a nis nach robh e a leith cho cas 's a bhithinn fhein nan do thachair dhomh a bhith 'nam mhaighstir-sgoile.

Coma co dhiubh, cha robh mise riaraichte le cuisean aig an am. Shuidhich mi uair is uair 'nam inntinn gu 'n teichinn dhachaidh ; ach o'n a bha caolas eadar mi agus taigh m' athar, cha robh e idir furasda dhomh teicheadh. A bharrachd air sin, bha eagal orm gu'n gabhadh m' athair orm, agus gu 'n cuireadh e air m' ais do 'n sgoil mi.

An uair a thoisich na smaointeanan so ri greim a dheanamh air m' inntinn, cha robh mi idir cho math gu ionnsachadh mo leasan 's a b' abhaist dhomh. Dh' fhas mi cho coma dhe gach ni a bha 'm maighstir-sgoile ag iarraidh orm a dheanamh. Mu dheireadh thall thoisich am maighstir-sgoile ri bhith 'gabhail orm gu doirbh. Cha 'n fhoghnadh leis gabhail orm air na dearnachan, ach, le cead na cuideachd, air mo mhasan. Thamailtich so mi buileach glan, agus thuirt mi rium fhein nach fhanainn ni b' fhaide, ciod sam bith mar a thachradh dhomh an deigh dhomh falbh. Bha mi cho rag ris a' mhac-mhollachd. Bha, agus tha, mi ruadh ; agus tha e air a radh gu bheil na daoine ruadha rag. Shuidhich mi 'nam inntinn mu dheireadh gu feuchainn ri teicheadh dhachaidh cho luath 's a gheibhinn greim air te dhe na geolachan a bh' ann am Port a' Mhuilinn. Bha fhios agam nach b' urrainn domh

te seach te dhe na geolachan a chur a mach gun
chuideachadh, agus o'n a bha e 'nam bheachd teicheadh
gun fhios do 'n mhaighstir-sgoile cha robh agam ach a
bhith 'feitheamh gus am faighinn cothrom air te dhiubh a
thoirt leam an uair a bhiodh i air bhog.

Latha dhe na laithean dh' eirich mi gu math moch, agus
chunnaic mi dithis dhaoine 'direadh o'n chladach, agus iad
a' deanamh direach air an taigh aig Fear Stocaidh. Ghabh
mi sios thun a' chladaich far an do shaoil mi an d'thainig
na daoine air tir. Ciod a bha romham an sin ach geola
bheag, sgiobalta, 's i air bhog. Cho luath 'sa bh' agam
dh fhuasgail mi i, agus leum mi steach innte. Bu ghle
thoigh leam a bhith ann am bataichean a h-uile uair a
gheibhinn an cothrom, agus ged nach rachadh agam air
iomradh a dheanamh leis an da laimh, bha mi comasach
air beagan sgolaidh a dheanamh. Thug mi an aire gu robh
an soirbheas leam, agus thug se misneach nach bu bheag
dhomh. Ach ged a bha 'n soirbheas leam, bha sruth laidir
a' ruith eadar Stocaidh agus an t-Eilean-Tarsuinn, agus a
dh'aindeoin gach oidhirp a thug mi air cumail dluth ri
cladach an Eilean-Tarsuinn, thug an sruth agus a' ghaoth
gheola seachad air ceann an iar-dheas an Eilean-Tarsuinn.
An uair a chunnaic mi nach b'urrainn domh greim a
dheanamh air fearann sam bith, chaill mi mo mhisneach gu
buileach, agus thilg mi an ramh air urlar na geola, agus
bhuail mi air caoineadh. Bha mi gus mo thoiladh leis an
acras, oir cha d'ith mi greim bidh o'n a ghabh mi mo
shuipeir an oidhche roimhe sin. B' fhearr leam na na
chunnaic mi riamh mu choinneamh mo dha shul gu robh
mi gun charachadh a' Stocaidh. Ach cha deanadh
aithreachas feum 'san am. An uair a bha mi sgith caoinidh
thuit mi 'nam chadal. Gu fortanach bha 'n t-side briagha,
blath. An uair a dhuisg mi bha 'n oidhche dhubh ann,
agus leis a' ghluasad a bh' air a' gheolaidh dh' aithnich mi
gu robh mi fada mach 's a' chuan. Bhuail an t-eagal mi.
Thoisich mi ri smaointean gu faodadh muc-mhara tighinn
an uachdar, agus mi fhein agus a' gheola itheadh a dh' aon

ghreim. Uair eiginn mu'n d' thainig an latha thuit mi 'nam chadal. Cha 'n urrainn dhomh a radh ciod an uine a bha mi 'nam chadal anns a' gheolaidh ; ach an uair a dhuisg mi, ciod a b' iongantaiche leam na bhith 'nam laidhe ann an leabaidh bhig a bh' ann an seomar beag, dorcha. Bha mi greis mhor 'nam dhusgadh mu'n do thuig mi c' aite an robh mi. Cha robh mi 'cluinntinn fuaim sam bith a bheireadh orm a thuigsinn co dhiubh a bha mi air muir no air tir. Bha mo cheann car na bhreislich co dhiu. Ged nach robh mi a' tuigsinn mar a bha mi aig an am, tha 'chuis coltach gu robh mi fada o bhith slan. B' e so a' cheud fhaothachadh a fhuair mi o'n tinneas a bh' orm san am.

Tha cuimhne gle mhath agam gu'n cuala mi coiseachd os mo chionn, agus thuig mi gur ann air bord luinge a bha mi. Sheall mi mu'n cuairt orm ni b' fhearr, agus an sin dh' aithnich mi gur ann 'san toll-thoisich a bha mi 'nam laidhe. An uair a bha mi 'fuireach ann an Stocaidh bha mi uair is uair air bord te no dha dhe na soithichean a bhiodh aig acair' anns an acarsaid, an uair a bhiodh a' ghaoth 'nan aghaidh a' dol troimh 'n chaolas ; agus thug fear dhe na seoladairean do 'n toll-thoisich mi. B' e so a thug orm a thuigsinn gur ann 'san toll-thoisich a bha mi 'nam laidhe.

An uine gun bhith fada chuala mi neach a' tighinn a nuas far an robh mi 'nam laidhe. Bha am beagan soluis a bha 'tighinn troimh 'n uinneig bhig a bha os cionn an t-seomair air thuar a bhith gu buileach air falbh ; oir b' e am feasgar anamoch a bh' ann. Cha b' urrainn mi dheanamh a mach ach gur e firionnach a thainig do'n t-seomar. Thug e cuairt no dha air feadh an t-seomair mar gu'm biodh e ag iarraidh rud eiginn a bh' air chall air. Thug e ceum a nall gu taobh na leapadh anns an robh mi 'nam laidhe, agus chuir e a chluas os cionn m' analach, mar gu'm biodh e air son fios fhaotainn an robh an anail sios is suas annam. Ghrad thionndaidh e air a shail, agus ghabh e suas air an fharadh 'na dheannamh. Cha robh e fada air falbh an uair a thill e agus solus aige. Ach, a mhic chridhe, an uair a chunnaic mise aogasg agus

cruth an duine ri solus a' chruisgein, cha mhor nach do
leum an t-anam asam. Bha a chraicionn cho dubh ris a'
phoit, agus bha a dha shuil cho geal ris a' chaile; agus ar
leam gu robh lainnir asda mar gu'm biodh a suilean cait-
fhiadhaich. Bha beul air anns an rachadh mo cheann, ar
leam; agus chuireadh am boras agus na spreilean a bh' air
eagal air dearg mheirleach! An uair a chunnaic e gu robh
mo shuilean fosgailte, agus mi ag amharc air ann an clar
an aodainn, chuir e drein air mar gu'm biodh e 'dol 'gam
itheadh; ach ma chuir, cha 'n fhaca mise riamh a leithid a
dh' fhiaclan ann an ceann creutair cruthaichte! Chlisg an
cridhe agam; oir shaoil mi gur e an droch spiorad a bh' ann
a' tighinn air mo thoir. Chuala mi gu'm biodh an droch
spiorad far am biodh daoine a' cluich air chairtean; agus
leis cho fior dheidheil 's a bha mi fhein air a bhith far am
biodh iad a' cluich air na cairtean, thuirteadh iomadh uair
rium gu'n tigeadh an droch spiorad air mo thoir latha no
latha eiginn, agus gu sguabadh e leis 'na fhinean mi gu
ruige an droch aite. Thug mi seorsa de ghlaodh asam,
agus shiolaidh mi seachad ann an neul. An uair a dhuisg
mi as an neul bha dithis no triuir dhaoine timchioll orm aig
an leabaidh, agus iad an deigh a bhith 'crathadh uisge orm,
agus a' cur arain air a losgadh ri mo shroin, a chum mo
thoirt as an neul. 'Nam measg so bha am fear dub'n,
duaichnidh a chlisg an cridhe agam mu'n deachaidh mi
anns an neul. An uair a chunnaic mi e ann am measg
chaich, dh'aithnich mi gur e duine saoghalta' bh' ann. Co a
bh' ann, ma ta, ach an duine dubh a bha 'na chocaire air
an t-soitheach. Cha 'n fhaca mise duine dubh riamh
riomhe; agus ged a chuala mi gu math tric iomradh air
d'oine dubha, cha do shaoil mi ga'm biodh iad 'nan seoladairean, no idir 'nan cocairean air soithichean anns an
rioghachd so.

Ann am beagan uine dh' fhas mi cho math 's gu robh
mi comasach air eirigh agus a dhol gu bord an t-soithich a
h-uile latha. Bha gach aon a bha air an t-soitheach gle
chaoimhneil rium. Cha robh a h-aon dhiubh ni bu

chaoimhneile rium na 'n duine dubh. Mar bu trice bhithinn
ag obair dha mar a b' urrainn agus a b' aithne dhomh.
Cha robh aige ach an droch Bheurla, agus cha b' i mo
Bheurla-sa moran a b' fhearr.

An uair a dh' fhas mi laidir, chuir an sgiobair, air latha
araidh, fios orm do 'n chabin, agus dh' fheoraich e dhiom
cia mar a chaidh m' fhuadach o 'hir anns a' gheolaidh.
Dh' innis mi dha gu saor, soilleir mar a thachair dhomh o
thoiseach gu deireadh.

" Ma ta," ars' esan, " ma ghabhas tu mo chomhairle-sa
bidh tu gu brath tuilleadh umhail do gach aon aig am bi
thu mar sheirbhiseach.   Cha 'n fhaodar an toil fhein a
thoirt do d' leithid-sa de bhalach og idir.   Feumaidh tu a
bhith gle umhail fad 's a bhios tu air bord 's an luing so.
Faodaidh tu iomadh cuideachadh a dheanamh leis na
lamhan, agus leis a' chocaire.   Cha deanar ainneart sam
bith ort.   Gheibh thu do shath de 'n bhiadh, agus an uair a
ruigeas sinn a' cheud bhaile-puirt gheibh thu deise aodaich,
ma bhios tu modhail, iomchuidh, glic, dichiollach, deanad-
ach.   Ach mo thruaighe do chor, a laochain, mur bi thu
umhail, easgaidh. Ma theannas a h-aon do na seoladairean
ri eucoir a dheanamh ort, ruig mise, agus cha 'n eagal dhut.
Ach bi air d' fhaicill nach dean thu an lideadh a's lugha de
bhreig, ar neo ma ni, theid do thilgeadh an coinneamh do
chinn leis a' chliathaich.   Tha mise 'dol leis an luchd a th'
agam air bord gu ruige Cadis anns a' Spainn.   Aig an
fhortan mhor a tha fios caite an teid an long na dheigh
sin.   An uair a ruigeas mi am baile-puirt cuiridh mi litir
gu d' athair, no thun a' mhaighstir a tha os cionn d' athar,
a dh'innseadh gu bheil thu gu sabhailte air bord an so.
Tha fhios agam gu 'm bi d' athair agus do mhathair a'
caoidh gu trom 'nad' dheigh."

Faodaidh mi radh gu robh mi fhein agus na scoladairean cho reidh 's a dh' iarradh duine sinn a bhith.   Bha
mise deonach air ni sam bith a dheanamh a dh' iarradh
iad orm.   Fhuair mi mach o'n uair ud gu 'n d' thug an
sgiobair ordugh teann dhaibh gun iad a dheanamh eucoir

sam bith orm. Bha mi gu nadurr gle mhisneachail, agus cha ghabhainn miapadh sam bith an uair a bhithinn ann an cunnart. Thug so air na seoladairean meas a bharrachd a bhith aca orm.

Thachair aimsir gle fhabharrach ruinn gus an d' rainig sinn Cadis. Cha robh sinn a bheag de laithean an deigh an luchd a bh' againn air bord fhaotainn bhar ar laimh, an uair a fhuair sinn luchd eile air bord air son a dhol leis gu ruige Ceann a' deas America. B' e fion a' chuid bu mho de 'n luchd a bh' againn air bord. Comhladh ris a so bha min mhin, gran, olla, agus frasan dhe gach scorsa againn mar an ceudna air bord.

Rinn an sgiobair rium mar a gheall e. An uair a fhuair e an luchd air bord thug e leis mi do 'n bhaile, agus cheannaich e deise dhomh cho math 's a bha riamh agam. Agus thug e dhomh mar an ceudna gach aodach cuim a bha dhith orm, gus am paighinn e le mo chosnadh. Bha mi cho spaideil ri mac mathar a bh'air bord. Rinn mi fastadh ris an sgiobair, agus bha mo bhiadh agus mo thuarasdal agam mar a bh'aig fear eile dhe na seoladairean. Cha robh an tuarasdal ach beag ; ach bu mhath e. Bha mi suidhichte gu 'n cuirinn a' cheud tuarasdal bliadhna a choisninn, cearta, cruinne, comhladh a dh' ionnsuidh m' athar agus mo mhathar. Faodaidh mi radh gu robh mi aig an am suidhichte nach caithinn sgillinn de mo thuarasdal ann an goraiche, no ann an ceannach nithean gun fheum. Bha meas mor agam air an sgiobair, agus thuirt mi rium fhein gu feuchainn, cha'n e mhain ri 'chomh-airle a ghabhail, ach mar an ceudna ri bhith cho measarra ris anns gach doigh.

Beagan laithean mu'n do sheol sinn a Cadis gu ruige Ceann a' deas America, thug an sgiobair cead dhomh fhein agus do Naro, an Cocaire, a dhol sgriob air feadh a' bhaile, agus a mach thun na duthcha. Dh' fhalbh sinn beagan an deigh mheadhon latha, agus an deigh dhuinn beagan uine a chur seachad anns a' bhaile, thug sinn ar n-aghaidh air an duthaich. B' e sin an duthaich a tha maiseach. Cha ghabh

—

e innseadh, agus idir cha ghabh e tuigsinn, ged a theann-
ainnse ri min-chunntas a thoirt dhuibh. Bha leithid de
chraobhan de gach seorsa a' tachairt ruinn mar a bha sinn
a' dol air ar n-aghaidh troimh 'n duthaich. Bha an latha
anabarrach blath, mar a tha 'n aimsir an sid an comhnuidh
mu 'n am ud de 'n bhliadhna. Bhuail am pathadh sinn,
agus ged nach robh annas sam bith againn de mheasan,
bha sinn gu mor a' miannachadh beagan de na bh' air cuid
dhe na craobhan a bhith againn. Ach bha eagal oirnn
gu 'n cuirteadh ann am priosan sinn nam faighteadh sinn
a' toirt air falbh nam measan. Coma co dhiu, leis a h-uile
suil is miannachadh a bh' againn air na measan, 's ann a
chomhairlich Naro dhomh fhein a dhol a steach do phairc
anns an robh moran mheasan, agus lan mo phocaidean a
thoirt leam dhiubh. Mar a bha 'ghoraiche agus cion toirt
fa near orm, ghabh mi a chomhairle. An uair bha gu leor
air thuar a bhith agam, thainig dithis dhaoine gun fhios
orm, mar gu 'n tigeadh iad a nios as an talamh, agus rug
iad air amhaich orm. Cha robh mise a' tuigsinn aon
fhacal dhe na bha iad ag radh, ach bha e furasda gu leor
dhomh a thuigsinn gu robh lan an cinn de chorruich orra.
Thug iad fior dhroch fhasgadh air an amhaich agam, agus cha
mhor nach'eil mi cinnteach gu'n do chuir iad an t-anam asam
leis an eagal nan do thachair dhomh a bhith leam fhein.
Cho luath 's a bha 'na chnamhan leum Naro far an robh mi,
agus mhaoidh e gu fiadhaich air na fir aig an robh greim
orm. Dh' fhas iad moran ni bu shiobhalta rium an uair
sin. Bha Spainish gu leor aig Naro, agus chumadh e facal
riutha gun taing dhaibh. Be cheud ni a bhuail 's a' cheann
aige gu 'n tugadh e ruith phronnaidh air an dithis aca, agus
gu 'n teicheamaid le cheile do'n bhaile; ach thug e an aire
gu robh dithis no triuir eile cluth air laimh, agus thuig e
nach deanadh lamhachas-laidir feum sam bith dhuinn.
Thairg e mu dheireadh suim airgid a thoirt dhaibh nan
leigeadh iad as mi. Sid rud nach deanadh iad air chor
sam bith. Dh' fhalbh iad leam gus mo thoirt thairis do
fhear de mhaoir an lagha. Lean Naro mi a' h-uile ceum

gus an d' rainig sinn an t-aite anns an robh am breitheamh
'na shuidhe. An uair a chuireadh 'na lathair mi dh' aidich
mi gu saor gu robh mi ciontach, ach cha d' aidich mi idir
gu robh Naro 'gam bhrosnachadh gus a dhol a ghoid 'nam
measan. An uair a chuala 'm breitheamh mar a bha 'chuis
dhit e mi, agus dh' orduich e mo ghleidheadh ann am
priosan fad seachduin, mur paighinn fhein, no neach eile
air mo shon, deich buinn airgid de chain. Cha robh
agamsa ris an t-saoghal ach da bhonn. Cha do thachair a
bhith aig Naro ach na dheanadh mu choig buinn. Cha
robh fios againn ciod a dheanamaid. Thuirt am breitheamh
gu 'n tugadh e d il seachad gus am faigheadh Naro an
t-airgiod ; ach thuirt e gu feumadh bonn airgid a bhith air
a phaigheadh air son a' h-uile uair an uaireadair a bhiodh
Naro gun tighinn, agus mur biodh e air ais aig a' phriosan
aig uair araidh, gu 'm biodh am priosan air a dhunadh, agus
nach rachadh 'fhosgladh gu deich uairean an la-iar-na-
mhaireach.

An uair a chuala Naro so ghrad dh' fhalbh e feuch am
faigheadh e an t-airgiod. Chuireadh mise ann an seomar
beag, fuar, dorcha a bha ann am fior iochdar a' phriosain ;
ach ma chuir, cha mhor nach do bhrist mo chridhe. Chaoin
mi cinneadh mo sheanamhar. Bha eagal orm gu marbh-
adh na Spainich mi mu'n tigeadh Naro air ais leis an
airgiod. B' fhearr leam na na chunnaic mi riamh mu
choinneamh mo dha shul gu robh mi fo riaghladh a'
mhaighstir-sgoile ann an Stocaidh. An uair a bha mi sgith
caoinidh sguir mi. Bha mi 'faireachadh na h-uine anabarrach
fada. Mu dheireadh thainig an oidhche, agus dh' aithnich
mi nach robh agam ach a bhith anns a' phriosan gu an
tigeadh na deich uairean an la-iar-na-mhaireach.

Cha bu luaithe dh' fhas an oidhche dorcha na thoisich na
rodain air tighinn do 'n t-seomar. Ach mа thoisich, chur
iad barrachd eagail orm na bha riamh roimhe orm. Cha 'n
fhaca mise rodain riamh a bha cho dana riutha. Tha mi
'lan-chreidsinn gu'n itheadh iad beo mi nan do leig mi
leotha. Cha 'n 'eil cunntas air na thainig do 'n t-seomar

dhiubh. Thigeadh iad an drasta 'sa rithist a chriomadh nam brog agam. Cha robh agam mu dheireadh ach seasamh air seorsa de dh' aite suidhe a bh' anns an t-seomar agus mo dha laimh a chur ann am pocaidean na briogais, agus a bhith 'crathadh te ma seach dhe mo chasan gun fhois air eagal gu rachadh a h-aon de na creutairean granada suas ann an osan na briogais agam.

Gu fortanach cha robh an oidhche ach goirid. An uair a thoisich solus an latha ri tighinn do 'n t-seomar is ann a chunnaic mi an seorsa chompanach a bh' agam fad na h-oidhche. Bha ann an sin laoisg eagalach de rodain mhora, bhlara, dhubha. Cha robh a' bheag a dh' fhiamh no dh' eagal aca romham. Thug mi suil mu'n cuairt dhomh feuch am faicinn ni sam bith a dheanadh slacan leis an cuirinn an t-eanchain a' grunnan dhiubh, agus gu fortanach chaidh agam air sgealb mhath a thoirt as an t-seorse cathrach air an robh mi 'nam sheasamh fad na h-oidhche. Thug mi an aire gu robh an aireamh bu mho dhiubh a' tighinn a mach agus a' dol a steach air aon fhear dhe na tuill. An uair a chunnaic mi gu robh moran dhiubh air tighinn a mach, thug mi leum thun an tuill, agus thoisich mi air gabhail dhaibh cho math 's a b' urrainn mi. Tha fhios agam gu 'n do leon mi moran dhiubh, ach cha do ghrad mharbh mi ach na coig dhiubh. Shuidh mi air a' chathair, agus an uine ghoirid thuit mi 'nam chadal. Tha fhios agam nach robh mi moran uine 'nam chadal ; ach an uair a dhuisg mi cha robh fear dhe na coig rodain mharbha nach robh air an toirt air falbh. Tha mi cinnteach gu 'n d' thug na beistean eile leotha iad gus an itheadh.

[RI LEANTUINN].

A STRANGE REVENGE.

By D. NAIRNE.

CHAPTER XVI.

DRAMATIC EVENTS.

IN a half dazed, aimless condition of mind, David had almost reached his own apartment when it suddenly occurred to him that it was his duty to inform the laird of what had transpired in Flora's chamber. As yet he had formed no coherent idea of what the Witch's strange behaviour meant. The vision, or whatever it was, that had dismissed him from the room held his mind in a thraldom of wonderment. He was not afraid. Terror inspiring as the circumstances appeared, he groped his way along the dark passages and up the narrow winding stairs without light and without a single nervous thought intruding itself upon him.

What David would have told the Laird was never known; for he found himself in another chamber of death! Never, in the whole course of his life, did he allude to that ultramundane experience; but it occurred to John occasionally that he had more respect for the ghost lore of the district than was his wont, certainly his studies were much confined to psychical and psychological subjects.

The lamps burned brightly in the laird's room, revealing him extended on a couch as if he had fallen asleep in the act of reading the letter which lay on the floor by his side. Knowing that his father was a light sleeper, David called him, asking why he was not in bed at that late hour of the night. There was no response; and suddenly the conviction seized him that there was the silence of death in the room! With a cry, he sprang forward and seized the drooping hand, only to find that it was stiff, cold, and clammy.

At the terrible discovery, David trembled as an aspen leaf in the breeze, and sank helpless upon the floor, for a time mercifully beyond reach of the brain-shattering grief and terror which must have crushed him. To be confronted with a revelation from the unseen, and then with death itself, in a few brief minutes, was an experience beyond the limits of ordinary endurance ; and it was one from the effects of which David never absolutely recovered.

And so it proved that the Professor had been more successful, in one respect, in his revengeful stratagems than he intended. For the letter on the floor was in his handwriting, and the shock it gave, acting on a diseased heart, had terminated the laird's earthly career sooner than nature had planned. When Richard reached Edinburgh, he did not observe that his arrival had been watched by Professor Somerton, nor that the Professor at once hurried towards the departing mail for the North, and deposited a letter with the guard. This was what he wrote :—

" Probably—I would almost say certainly—you will have forgotten the incident in your early life which it is now my peculiar pleasure to recall to your memory. During the short period I have been your neighbour, you have known me as Professor Somerton. No doubt, you considered me a very unsocial neighbour ; but when you read my signature, which, perhaps, you have done already, you will quite agree with me that, in the circumstances, I could be nothing else.

" If you still possess among your literary curiosities the unique note I wrote you on a certain occasion which need not be more definitely alluded to ; please refer to its terms. I wrote—in my own blood—that I would have revenge though I should wait a lifetime for the luxury of it. During these long years you doubtless have, many a time, chuckled over the emptiness of that threat. But that only shews that you underestimated the manner of man with whom you had to deal.

" I have been patient ; but you will endorse the old saw that all things come to those who wait. My revenge has come ; and time has not dulled my appetite for its proper enjoyment. In its character it has exceeded my expectations. I have passed a most profitable holiday, nursing my hatred of you—which has in no way diminished—and planning the wrecking of your household. Things were too Devilishly pleasant for you—I should not have written that word, with a big D, too ; for, above all things, I prefer to be courteous with my pen ; but now that it is written, you had better swallow it.

"To the point : although in Edinburgh, and while I have received no tidings of your affairs since I left, I can picture your circumstances in a single sentence. The girl you call Flora is dead ; your wretched heart is sore with grief ; and your son and heir is off to lark it a bit in this gay city. Excellent arrangement, isn't it ?

" I have something to tell you which will, as the phrase conveniently goes, wring your withers.

" *The girl Flora has been poisoned, and the murderer is your son and heir, Richard !* He has committed the deed with the object of gaining my daughter's hand—silly fool ; simple dupe. Nature could not have provided me with a better instrument whereby to ruin you. And here allow me to explain that I had the pleasure of supplying him — at his own request—with the means necessary to send his sweetheart to a premature grave.

" For various reasons, I do not intend to inform the criminal authorities of what has taken place, because I guess you will be broken enough without having your unworthy son despatched by the hangman. You need not write thanking me for shewing you this small degree of consideration.

" As I have no prospect of meeting you again in this earthly sphere, I had better say farewell, with the hope of *seeing* you—excuse me, but I have no particular desire for a *meeting* - in the hottest corner of the next world.

" If it will in any way add to your wretchedness, I may as well explain that the poison the girl swallowed is so

2

slow in its working that she may probably be buried alive. There is only one antidote, and nobody but myself knows who possesses the secret.

" Farewell ; we are quits, curse you, with, you will allow, somewhat of an advantage on the side of

" CHRISTOPHER WALSH."

.   .   .   .

One! two! three!   It is the Castle bell solemnly pealing!   Half-sleeping people start up in bed at the sound, consult their clocks, and conclude that, after all, they must have been dreaming.   Others, more certain of their wakefulness, peer in a terrified way out at door and window in the direction of the Castle, and with a prayer to be protected against the influences of the uncanny, resume their slumbers.   Within the Castle itself, the sound of the bell gave rise to a scene of consternation and superstitious terror.   Wrapped in sheets, blankets, and other convenient coverings, the servants, male and female, rushed to John's room, and huddled together like cattle in a thunderstorm.

When the bell ceased, their superstitious fright was intensified tenfold by a shriek, shrill and loud, that penetrated every part of the building; then there was a crash of glass—and then silence !

It was mad Elspeth's freak in celebration of her self-sought death !

The Witch had indeed gone crazy ; but, in some measure, there was, as the saying goes, method in her madness.   Haunted (by the terrors of the imagination ; or by actual apparition, who knows?) into the impulse to administer the antidote, and so, despite her solemn oath to the Professor, save Flora's life, she had reasoned that her own would not be worth one hour's purchase once the true state of matters became known ; and, weary of persecution, shunned by every man, woman, and child in the district, weary, too, of evil doing, she resolved to give a life and take her own—carrying to the grave with her the secret of those wonderful herbal mixtures which could, as it were, suspend life and revive it again! The age for burning witches had now passed; but probably she was right — she would, when the circumstances became public, have been hounded to death like a fox. What necessity for reasoning the philosophy of the matter? Further than saying that it was a singular piece of providence that which placed poor Elspeth under a debt of obligation to Flora, and so brought about the circumventing of a piece of wicked and treacherous villainy.

Once her mission to the Castle had been accomplished, and the conviction overcame her with irresistible force that nothing now remained but the fatal plunge into the river. Strange freak it was, but she shuddered at the thought of making her exit from the world in silence, with no fellow human being aware that something unusual was happening. Knowing the Castle well, she seized the lamp and hurried to the bell rope, laughing hysterically at the thought of alarming Castle and countryside. Making her escape by the window through which she had entered (which crashed down after her), the demented creature rushed, gesticulating and incoherent, in the direction of the water. Where the recent flood had scooped out the bank, the current slowed itself into a pool, deep and inky, under the shadow of the fir plantation; then danced away merrily, fretting and foaming among boulders, glad again of the more picturesque life.

There was a hurried rustle among the bushes; a cry of human despair that sent the four-footed beasts abroad scampering to their holes; a plunge; and Elspeth the Witch had penetrated the great secret of death!

"The Witch is drowned," was all people said when the water threw up its dead. Not a single eye moistened, no lips framed an expression of sympathy—such a life were better ended, surely; but whose the right to pronounce the judgment?

"Come awa' an' see the maister," John was saying to the frightened group of servants, "if the world's comin' tae an end, there's nae use gaun tae sleep. Sudden deaths, daft Witch's runnin' aboot the hoose at the dead o' nicht, bells ringin', screechin', an' window smashin'—it's enough tae drive a body clean daft."

"He'll better tak' my warnin' the noo," said the table-maid, with teeth a-chatter, "I canna bide in a hunted hoose at the wages I get."

"I aye thocht the Castle was haunted," ventured the cook, "the place is auld and eerie, and I've heard gey queer soonds at nicht."

"My door opened itsel' ae nicht last week," volunteered the kitchen-maid, "an' I thocht there was a rustlin' kind o' soond."

"The black cat ran intae the kitchen ae nicht, wi' its back up an' half dead wi' fricht—they say black cats can see ghosts," whispered the maid of all work.

And so the simple people brewed their own fears until in desperation, John marshalled the procession — each carrying a light, and several armed with poker, tongs, and other lethal weapons, for the heroic vanquishing of the spirits—to the laird's apartment. When they reached the room, David had just regained consciousness. With head elbowed up, he was trying to realise what had happened ; when, before he could reply to the peremptory knocking, the door opened, and the grotesque and ghostly-looking company crowded hurriedly in, glad to escape from the darkness without.

The Laird dead ! Such an awful realisation of their superstitious fears petrified them so much that David had to make repeated appeals for a little brandy and water before John found himself capable of movement. Thus revived, he suddenly recollected that he had left the Witch in Flora's chamber. What had taken place ? He walked, unsteadily, towards the door, and then paused. Could he venture in there again ? At the full recollection of what had occurred, his face grew paler still, his legs shook, and he sank powerless upon a chair.

"Go some of you to Miss Flora's room," he said, "and tell me if the Witch is still there."

But he might as well have asked John and the rest of them to throw themselves from the Castle turrets. They shrank back and clutched each other, at the bare idea of bearding the Witch in such awful circumstances.

"Then follow me," cried David, pulling himself together —and panic stricken, they followed.

His hand shook as he turned the handle of the door; he flung it open, and found the room in darkness.

"Hold up the lights!" he cried, "Merciful heavens, what is this?"

Scattered about the floor were the cerement cloths in which Flora's body had been wound; the shattered fragments of a small bottle lay about, and the room was filled with the smell of some unfamiliar drug.

"Bring in the lights," he commanded in a hoarse whisper, and all eyes were turned, terror stricken, upon the bed.

"My God!"

It was David's voice; and the words were uttered fervently, as if an appeal to Heaven for an explanation of the night's mysteries.

Flora lay comfortably tucked in, in a deep slumber, breathing heavily; nature, it seemed to the onlooker, was labouring to work off a heavy incubus. Her face was pale and sunken; but there was life—blessed life!

"She lives!"

With that cry David fell upon his knees at the bed side. John and the others involuntarily followed his example, speechless with wonder. Then after a while, a solemn-toned voice filled the chamber—a voice that spoke from a heart thrilled with awe, reverence, and thankfulness.

It was John rehearsing all he knew in that line—the Lord's prayer.

CHAPTER XVII.

AN UNBROTHERLY ACT.

A SOLITARY figure strode along the road in the darkness. His step was weary ; his manner nervous. Now and again an approaching step alarmed him, and he would crouch behind a bush or get behind a tree until the danger of recognition had passed. He was evidently well acquainted with the locality, for when within half-a-mile of the Castle, he took to the fields, and easily made his way by ditch and gateway in its direction. A shepherd's cottage stood a little to the right of the route he was pursuing, with a bright light in the window ; a signal, perhaps, to the guid-man of the house to hurry home for supper. The solitary one hesitates a few minutes, and then cautiously approaches the cottage, having first made certain that the lighted apartment, though the peat fire burns brightly with a new replenishing, is empty.

As he pulls out and eagerly examines the dial of his watch, the rays of the lamp fall upon the face and figure of Richard Stuart ! But what a change has been wrought in his appearance since he left the Castle—his father's blessing ringing in his ears—on that eventful night. Travel-stained, haggard, and haunted-looking, it seemed that ten years and more had been added to his age within the space of a few days.

" Too early yet," he muttered to himself, as he turned away. " I must not risk meeting anyone in the Castle but David."

What a home-coming for the erstwhile gay, dashing young laird, whose name was that night in everybody's mouth ! As David had enjoined that John and his fellow-servants were not, on pain of instant dismissal, to mention that the Witch had paid a midnight visit to the Castle, the people of the district knew nothing more of the case than that Flora had miraculously recovered ; and now that the old laird was dead, they rejoiced that one whom they all loved and trusted so much had been brought, as it were, back from the grave to be the helpmeet of his successor. Thus was their sorrow tempered by a feeling of joy.

What momentous issues hang upon trifles! The exclamation is ever recurring in human history. Had Richard, instead of avoiding contact with his neighbours this night, met with and spoken to but one of them, the whole course of his life would inevitably have been changed from what it was now destined to be; perhaps, also, the extinction of the Stuart family would have been averted!

Sitting down at the edge of the fir wood, he buried his face in his hands, and gave himself up to reflection. His thoughts were bitter. Fate seemed to have turned its hand inexorably against him On his way across the Grampian hills, his horse had twice broken down, and ultimately, after trudging on foot for several hours, he had perforce to wait about half a day for the mail coach.

When he reached Inverness, the local paper informed him in a sympathetic paragraph that Miss Flora had, to the great sorrow of the entire community, expired suddenly, on the night of his departure from the Castle. Even had the Professor spoken the truth, the time had now expired for the successful administering of the antidote, did he possess the secret of it, which he did not. What, he asked himself in a startled way, might not the next paragraph in that same paper be—"Apprehension of Richard Stuart for murder!"

Half mad with the thought, he avoided the glare of the streets, and stole into the country. He felt that, with such a conscience, he dared not meet a known face. All he wished for was to explain to his brother that, dreadful as were the consequences, he had been the innocent dupe of their father's unscrupulous enemy.

After that, it remained for him that he now fully determined upon but to exile himself, track his cruel betrayer, and have the satisfaction of a tragic act of vengeance.

Recovered somewhat from the prostration that had followed the events of the night, David was also, at this moment, in a reflective mood. In what spirit, he was asking himself, should he meet his misguided brother, provided he had the courage to venture home after the heinous sin he had committed. Not a living soul, he supposed, knew the contents of the Professor's letter, but that individual and himself, and when he placed it in the fire, as he intended to do, all trace of Richard's crime would be destroyed. The Witch had evidently been mixed up in the affair, but for her own sake she was not likely to bruit it abroad ; he would make that sure, at all events, by seeing her and throwing out a threat. Should he, in these circumstances, and in order to avoid scandal, be charitable and forgiving ! Flora (who was still in bed, but recovering fast under the doctor's care) knew nothing except that she had been ill for a few days, and had been the victim of terrible dreams ; and eventuate what might, she must never learn the unpleasant secret. The knowledge of it would blight her life, and would not probably advance his suit. Would it not be best, then, to get Richard home, bury the past for ever, and let things run in the old groove ?

Somehow, this charitable view of the case did not appear to harmonise with David's frame of mind. Richard might come back repentant, and his old love be re-kindled; but what right had he to the heart and hand of a woman he had tried to murder ? As he asked himself the question, he started up with flashing eye and paced the room. It was only justice that he should suffer for his misdeeds—for a crime which tainted the family honour, and rendered him unfit for the company of honest men, far less to marry Flora, a princess among womankind.

" There are the proofs," he said aloud, in the excitement of his thoughts, and smiting the Professor's letter between his two hands, " the proofs of my brother's wickedness · is

it not my duty to spurn him, threaten him, send him forth never to show face again within these walls ; and then—"
He paused, and the blood shot up into his hot temples. Leaning an arm on the mantelpiece, he gazed into the fire with unwinking eyes, and his passion subsided into an expression of questioning doubt.

"After all, would Flora ever care for me—marry me ? "
He did not venture to answer the question, but stood there for a time in silent reverie. Then he started as the door was slowly opened.

Wheeling round, David was confronted with his brother!
The two men regarded each other in silence for a full minute—Richard, dejected in manner, eager to divine what his brother knew ; David, in surprise at his brother's changed appearance, and impressed by his guilty look, but at the same time feeling that his brother had come there to make some revelation. Now, when he thought of it, were the Professor's letter absolutely true, Richard could not have the fortitude to re-enter his home, even in this surreptitious way. Richard was the first to speak, and his voice trembled with emotion.

"Is it true ?" he asked
"That is a question which ought to come from me, not from you."

"Then you know all ?"
"I know what your *friend* Professor Somerton has written—he says you poisoned Flora."

"It's a lie—a cursed lie ! Is he not done with me yet, the villain ! It was he, the black-hearted swindler, under the cloak of doing a philanthropic act, that got me to administer the powder. He is the real murderer ; I have been but the ignorant, ill-fated, and blatant fool who carried out his behests, under an innocent misapprehension."

"A philanthropic act ; what do you mean ?" David queried, adopting a calm, judicial attitude.

"Well may you ask ; now when I think of the way in which I was deluded, I must have been mad, absolutely mad."

" None but a madman would do what you have done ; I wish you had been no brother of mine."

" My God, I wish I had never seen the light of heaven— what am I to do ; what am I to do?"

While speaking, Richard had been standing at the back of the door, and now he leaned heavily against it, and pressed his temples, which were throbbing and aching. A light had sprung into David's eyes, a cruel malicious light, at the thought that his brother was unaware of Flora's recovery.

" Then you did not intend to kill her when you administered the powder, as you call it ?"

" Kill her !" exclaimed Richard springing forward, " Kill Flora ! Good Heavens, what a question ; what have I come to ? A thousand times would I have taken my own life than even think upon such a deed. Kill her !" and the tears rolled down his cheeks in great heavy drops, while his lips visibly quivered. " It was to save her pain, the pain of my desertion of her, that prompted me to obey the villain."

" You took very effectual means to achieve your object," said David, cynically.

" I see you don't know the whole circumstances," Richard replied more calmly ; " I do not wish to exculpate the part I took in the least, but when I explain you will see that I am not so blackhearted as you appear to think. This blackguard of a man posed as my friend and as the friend of humanity. He made me believe that he abhorred human suffering, and that he had discovered a medicine whereby human love passions could be so changed that the breaking of a promise would not break the heart. He pretended to demonstrate this by experiments on animals. If, he said, I could, by administering the powder to Flora, alleviate the suffering which would be caused by my proving false to her, I would get the hand of his daughter. In the moments of my blind infatuation, I risked it. And here I am, the contemptible tool of a man's revenge, an agent in the death of the woman I loved; a blighted life before me; nothing to live for but to get vengeance."

During this recital David's feelings underwent, for the moment, a sympathetic revolution. He saw clearly that his brother, simple, thoughtless, and impetuous, had been made the dupe of a cunning scoundrel; but at this declaration of Richard's love he again drew himself up. With such contrition, he hastily reflected, matters would be sure to resume the old groove; and he was not prepared to permit that. No, he was more worthy of Flora, and must win her for himself.

"Your story is different from what the Professor gives in this letter," he said, "still, the fact of your having been a simpleton does not minimise your guilt."

"That I will never seek to minimise while I live, which I hope will not be for long. Death, and the tortures of hell, are preferable to wandering about the earth with a burning conscience."

David turned away to hide his emotion. Was it fair, he asked himself, to keep secret the news of Flora's recovery? And there was the risk, the great risk, of Richard's making the discovery himself. But why should he not suffer the agonies for a while; and if he did make the discovery, the idea of giving him a fright would be a sufficient excuse.

"Does father know—what is in that letter?"

Richard started at the question; for in the selfishness of his thoughts he had actually become oblivious to the fact that the laird's death was alike a painful and an important factor in the matter.

"He received this letter, and——" Perceiving what a blow he was about to inflict, David did not finish the sentence.

"Speak, man, speak," commanded Richard breathlessly, "I am sure he is ill; it would make him ill."

"It killed him!"

"He is not dead? What? You are not speaking the truth; you are not mocking me with a horrible nightmare? Say it's not true; for the love of God and our mother, say it's not true?"

"It is true—I found father dead, with this letter on the floor beside him."

"Richard gazed at his brother in a dazed, incomprehensible way, and then reeled against the wall. He would have fallen had David not darted to his assistance and led him to a chair.

"Swallow this," David said, filling out some brandy into a tumbler, "hard travel and the sorrowfulness of these events have unnerved you. Rest a while; we have much to say yet."

Then he turned to the uncurtained window and looked out into the starlight. How brightly they twinkled above the darkness—emblems of hope, ever beckoning humanity on to grander things, a thousand living anchorages, as it were, of that life-giving faith in a hereafter, without which our existence would materialise down to the level of the brutes. But David was in no mood to learn lessons either of hope or charity from the eloquence of the starry heavens. Stirred as he was at the sight of his brother's soul torture, and believing, as he did now, that he had fallen a victim to the machinations of a revengeful scoundrel, and had not the remotest idea of committing actual crime—still, he argued again why should he not suffer, at least temporarily, for his folly? For one thing, come what may, Richard must not stay under the Castle roof that night! What reason David had for coming to that resolution he abstained from confessing to himself; perhaps he was ashamed at this moment to analyse his own feelings, or examine too closely whether it was not the meting out of a slight measure of justice so much as his own selfishness and love passion that were dictating his singular conduct.

"It were better so," said Richard, rousing himself from a train of thought.

"What were better so?"

"That father died suddenly; otherwise he would have died a slow lingering death over my misdeeds. Poor Dad!

But, oh, David, it's hard to think that he died believing me guilty of—of—murder. Surely, if Heaven means the revelation of what is true and good, it will not be hid from him that my heart is clear from taint of intentional sin in this matter. You do not believe, David, that I administered this potion (I gave it in a glass of wine before I left, being told that my absence was necessary for its efficacious working—what a blind fool I was!) that I gave it to Flora to —to—take away her life?"

"It is an extraordinary explanation that you give—truth is, as you make out, fifty per cent. stranger than fiction— but I will believe your story in preference to that told in this letter. It is a relief, as you may imagine, for me to do this. Still, you are sorely to blame—I warned you against the folly into which you drifted so idiotically. I thought you were above the credulousness of a servant girl."

"Is she buried?" he asked in a nervous whisper.

"No," and David give a sigh of relief that the question was one he could answer truthfully. But he must change the subject if his plan was not to fail ; the topic was becoming dangerous to concealment.

" You are now proprietor of Stuart ; what are you to do?" he asked.

"Leave this, the scene of my shame—oh, Father in Heaven, why should I have been made the cause of killing the two people I loved most on earth! I shall go mad ; I shall go mad. But not yet—not yet," he added with set teeth. "I will first scour the whole earth, if necessary, to find this man and—strangle him ! Then—then ——." His head drooped, as one who saw nothing but a vista of despair.

"I think it would be wise for you to stay away for a time at least," pursued David with calm cruelty, "one does not know what may happen. There, for instance, are the servants, they saw——" ; he drew himself up with a jerk, for the next word on his tongue, "witch," would have inevitably led to the exposure of the part he was playing.

"Does anybody know," asked Richard apprehensively, "I had forgot, has anything been discovered?"

"As far as I know, the secret lies between you and me, and this letter. I had better commit it to the flames in your presence, in case of accidents."

The two remained silent for some minutes; until the lobby clock slowly rung out the hour of eleven.

"Before I go, David," said Richard, rising and approaching his brother, "for I cannot sleep within these walls, within the home where I have been so happy," and his voice shook, "there are some things which must be said. Nobody saw me come here, and nobody must see me leave. But for the scandal of it, and the impossibility of being revenged, I would willingly, if necessary, expiate my offence in prison, but that must not be; don't you agree?"

"The idea is preposterous."

"I am, as you say, now proprietor of our estate, but I will only remain nominally so, to avoid any suspicion on the part of the people, or our Edinburgh agents. I will go straight back to Edinburgh, and in a few days, when the—the—funerals are over, I will arrange with Smith & Renny what is to be done during my absence. You will take charge of the estate, and draw the revenues, subject to a deduction which will be paid through the firm to me, for I cannot travel without money. There will be sufficient for all of us; but, of course, all the improvements contemplated by father must be stopped, in the meantime."

"How am I to account for your absence, particularly at this time?"

"That will be easily done. When I left it was under the pretence of being unwell, though it was only the excitement of my mad act that ailed me. It should be intimated that I am too ill to come north—and, I fear, that may really be the case. My brain throbs and feels fevered. Then I will be ordered to travel abroad for my health. The rest we will leave to fate."

"If you have been seen travelling, that scheme will

work badly," remarked David, anxious only to clear obstacles out of the way.

"There were no persons on the coach that I knew, and I scarcely think I was recognised in town ; at all events I spoke to no one—in the circumstances I avoided recognition ; and innocent though I feel, and unsuspicious as the public may be. I must not be recognised on my return journey."

"How do you propose to avoid that ?"

"By a disguise. You remember that costume which I wore at Lady Baillie's fancy ball ? It deceived everybody, and is not old fashioned enough to provoke remark ; you will find it in my wardrobe."

"Do you wish it at once ?"

"At once."

"What about food ? You look ill, and must have something to eat."

"Nothing."

"Eat," he continued, when David had left the room, "eat (he might have said and be merry), and dear Flora my true sweet Flora, lying dead—and through me ! Is it all a horrid dream, or have I been mad ? Father——" He fell upon his knees in mute, agonising appeal.

When David returned with the clothes, it was evident that he, too, had had a struggle with himself. He looked paler and more nervous, and his face twitched as he discovered his brother's attitude ; but he clenched his hands in firm determination.

"Now, brother, while I change, go saddle the mare quietly and tie it to the yew tree I must ride to Inverness, and you can easily find an excuse for the beast being there—we have lent it before to friends passing."

When he returned, David found Richard fully equipped in his disguise, and eager to be away.

"Now, dear brother, give me your hand."

They stood there, gazing into each other's eyes, without a word being spoken. Richard's was the look of a man who was saying a last farewell, and wished to imprint upon his brain the likeness of the only creature he believed it was now left for him to love. David, conscience smitten, was even now debating with himself whether or not he should confess that Flora was alive. And even in the awful tension of that moment he hesitated. "It is only a temporary absence," said the tempter; and he listened to it—"punish him a little."

Who will calculate the moral crimes a man is ready to commit for the love of a woman?

"David," said Richard, still clasping firm the hand he thought was true, "I have done you also a grevious injury, for you loved Flora? Start not, David, I knew your secret; and I reckoned you far more worthy of her than I ever possibly could be. I will not argue if that affected my foolish action or not. But I ask your forgiveness for destroying that—that which might have happened. Can you forgive your broken-hearted brother?"

"I have nothing to forgive," said David in a husky voice.

"Ay, you may say so," was the reply, "but the trembling of your hand confirms what I have said. Lead the way, David," he went on in a cheerier voice, "our school motto used to be Excelsior; mine is now Vengeance!"

At the door-step, before David could recover himself from a nervous stupor which had overcome him, Richard had given him a vehement embrace, and rushed down the path.

"Farewell!" he cried in agonised tones, "Farewell!"

For a moment or two David stood clutching his forehead, then he rushed forward with an hysterical cry.

"What have I done; what have I done? Richard! Richard! Come back! come back!"

But the only answer was a clatter of hoofs on the roadway.

"Here he is, in a dead faint," said John to a group of alarmed servants a little later, "get him in as fast as possible or he'll get his death o' cauld. Puir chield, perhaps he's seen anither ghaist."

[TO BE CONTINUED.]

SKYE BARDS.

BY MAGNUS MACLEAN, M.A., F.R.S.E.

Part III.

LADY D'OYLY.

BAINTIGHEARNA D'OYLY is a grand-daughter of John Macleod, ninth Laird of Raasay. He was the laird when Johnson and Boswell were there in their tour through the Western Isles. Mr Sinclair, Glasgow, published a collection of her songs with music not many years ago. Five of her songs appear in An t-Oranaiche.

1. Oran do Dh-Eilthireach.
2. Cumha Mhic-Leoid.
3. Oran do Phrionns' Tearlach.
4. Mo run air mo Leannan.
5. Oran Gaoil.

I shall quote two verses from her Oran Gaoil to show what, in her estimation, are the essential requisites in a lover :—

ORAN GAOIL, LE BAINTIGHEARNA D'OYLY.

Tha beul an oigeir mar bhilibh rosan,
'S a ghuth mar smeorach, no ceol nan teud,
Da bhlath-shuil mhiogach 'n a aghaidh mhin-gheal,
Mar it' an fhireun a mhala reidh.
Fear foinnidh dealbhach a shiubhal garbhlaich
Am beul an anamoich ri sealg an fheidh,
'S e caoidh do chomhraidh a dh-fhag fo bhron mi,
'S mi bhi gun choir ort, dh-fhag trom mo cheum.

Tha suil mo ruin-sa gu meallach ciuine,
'S mar dhearcag dhu-ghorm fo dhriuchd a' fas,
Mar ghrian ag eirigh moch maduinn Cheitin
Tha sealladh m' eudail gu h-eibhinn tlath ;

Do dheud geal direach fo'd bhilibh min-dhearg,
Am beul na firinn bho 'm millse failt',
Cha 'n iarrainn sugradh ach pog bho d' chur-bheul
Co riamh thug suil ort, 's a dhiult dhuit gradh ?

MURDO MACLEOD.

Murdo Macleod, son of Alexander Macleod, Triaslan, or Alasdair Og Thriaslan, was a bard of some repute in his own day. He emigrated to America about 1810, and I have been unable to find anything further about him. One of his songs, wrongly attributed to his father, is printed by Mackenzie in his Beauties. The song is entitled Oran Sugraidh, and is in the form of a dialogue between himself and his mother.

JOHN MACLEAN.

John Maclean, Waternish, a sailor, composed several songs, many of which are held in high repute in the west of Skye. Two of them appear in An t-Oranaiche.

1. Thug mi Gaol do'n t-seoladair.
2. A ho ro mo Mhairi Lurach.

The first is supposed to be composed by his sweetheart to himself, and the second is an answer, trying to allay her fears as to the inconstancy of her sailor sweetheart. I take two verses from Thug mi Gaol do'n t-seoladair :—

Gur lionmhor mais' ri aireamh
Air an armunn dh-fhas gun mheang,
Gu'n aithnichinn fein air faireadh thu,
'S tu ard air bharr nam beann :
Bu deas air urlar claraidh thu,
'N uair thairneadh tu 'n tigh-dhanns'—
Troigh chuimir am broig chluaiseinich
'S gach gruagach ort an geall !

Ach innsidh mise 'n fhirinn duibh—
Mur bheil mo bharail faoin,
Tha gaol nam fear cho caochlaideach—
'S e 'seoladh mar a ghaoith,
Mar dhriuchd air madainn Cheitin
'S mar dhealt air bharr an fheoir ;
Le teas na greine eiridh e
'S cha leir dhuinn e 's na neoil.

I take other two verses from A ho ro mo Mhairi
Lurach :—

> Bidh mo smuaintean anns gach am ort,
> Ged a be ann a'dol do'n chrann mi ;
> Chuir thu seacharan am cheann,
> 'S cha 'n amais mi air ceann nan rop.
>
> Bidh mi smaointeach ort a'm leaba,
> Bidh mi bruadar ort a'm chadal,
> Cha leig mi thu, 'ghaoil, as m' aire,
> Fhad 's tha mi air thalamh beo.

Mr Henry Whyte has given an excellent translation of
"Thug mi gaol do'n scoladair." As the song is long, I
shall only quote the translation of the two verses which I
gave in Gaelic :—

> Thy merits are so many, love,
>   I cannot on them dwell ;
> I'd know thee far on mountain heights,
>   Or coming down the dell ;
> When joining in the giddy dance,
>   Who can with you compare ?
> Thy form and movements elegant
>   Steal hearts from ladies fair !
>
> The truth to you I'll now unfold—
>   Oh, deem me not unkind !
> The love of man unsettled is
>   And restless as the wind ;
> Like dew, which, falling in the night,
>   Or at the break of day,
> Will flee before the noon-day glare
>   And quickly pass away.

I am tempted to quote the last verse, for were the
spirit there breathed more prevalent there would be fewer
breaches of promises, and hence fewer *actions* for breaches
of promises :—

> 'S ma s' ni e nach 'eil ordaichte
> Gu 'n comhlaich sinn gu brath,
> Mo dhurachd thu bhi fallain,
> 'S mo roghainn ort thar chaich !

Ma bhrist thu 'nis na cumhnantan,
'S nach cuimhne leat mar bha,
Guidheam rogha ceile dhuit
A's laidhe 's eirigh slan !

And if stern fate has ordered so
    That we shall meet no more ;
And if by thee forgotten are
    Our vows upon the shore ;
I'll pray that health and happiness
    May ever with thee stay,
A charming wife to comfort thee
    And cheer thee on thy way.

Is it because the Highland women are actuated by a spirit similar to this, or is it because Highland men are more constant in their affections, that fewer actions, population for population, occur in the Highlands than among Scotch Lowlanders or among Englishmen ?

NORMAN NICOLSON.

Norman Nicolson, Scorrabreck, near Portree, composed a good many nice songs. He was taken up for poaching, and in consequence emigrated to America, where he died some years ago. Most of his songs are lost, but the one he composed about the poaching incident appears in An t-Oranaiche, and is entitled

'S GANN GU'N DIRICH MI CHAOIDH.

Seisd—'S gann gu'n dirich mi chaoidh,
    Dh-ionnsuidh frithean a' mhonaidh,
    'S gann gu'n dirich mi chaoidh.

Thainig litir a Dun-Eidcann
Nach faodainn fhein nis dol do'n mhonadh,
        'S gann, &c.

Tha mo ghunna caol air meirgeadh,
Cha teid mi do'n t-seilg leis tuille.
        'S gann, &c.

Theid a chrochadh air na tairgnean
'S cha b'e sin leam 'aite fuireach.

ANGUS MACPHEE.

Angus Macphee, Glendale, composed several very good songs. One of his best known ones is in An t-Oranaiche :—

BATA PHORT-RIGH.

Ho ro hog i o hal dal o halo i
Ho ro hog i o hal dal o halo i
Ho ro hog i o hal dal o halo i
Aig meud mo mhulad, cha'n urrainn mi 'innsi!

Gur mis tha fo mhulad 's mi siubhal a' chuain,
'S mi falbh do na h-Innsean ri sid a's droch uair ;
Croinn bhi 'gan rusgadh, a's siuil 'gan toirt bhuainn
'S an long mhor air a leth-taobh 'si 'gleachd ris a
    chuan.

D. LAMONT.

D. Lamont,[1] a native of Skye, emigrated to British North America. Here his health broke down, and he came back to Skye again, where he composed the following verses :—

Some forty years, with all their ills,
Have come and are gone by,
Since last I saw my native hills—
The rugged hills of Skye.
I view again my childhood's home,
But now no home of mine,
The fields where I was wont to roam
In seasons of lang syne.

How sadly changed the little glen ;
Its gladness turned to gloom,
And friends that lived around me then
Laid in the silent tomb !
The brook still runneth in its course,
The tide doth ebb and flow,
But things have altered for the worse
Since forty years ago.

I see the sights that tourists seek,
Black hills and mountains high,
Where the Coolin's loftiest peak
Is towering to the sky ;

[1] Is this a brother to John Lamont, Edinbain, who composed Chuir iad an t-suil a Pilot leam? See An t-Oranaiche, page 150.

Those ancient cairns and craggy nooks
That trav'llers deem so fair—
But then what signify their looks
When one can't live on air?

I oft my residence did change,
And many a place I've been,
My native place seems now more strange
Than anywhere I've been;
My pockets being so scarce of crowns,
That no one will me know,
For I have had my ups and downs
Since forty years ago.

If round the coasts you take a peep,
From Oban to Portree,
You'll scarcely see but flocks of sheep
Where dwellings used to be;
The hardy, honest, Highland race
Now thrive in other climes,
Who had to leave their native place
Through dearth of former times.

JOHN GILLIES.

John Gillies was partner with late Mr Archibald
Sinclair, printer, Glasgow. He went to Australia in 1857.
In the following poem he describes his experiences:—

LITIR BHO IAIN MAC-GILL'-IOS' A NEW ZEALAND.

'N uair dh' fhag mi Albainn thuathach
Le cabhlach luath nan crannagan
Chaidh sinn tre theas a's fhuachd
A bha uamhasach ri tachairt orr';
'S ge b' iomadh tonn a bhuail sinn,
A bhagair falach cuain oirnn,
Thug Dia 'na throcair bhuan sinn
A steach o'n chuan do'n chala so.

" 'N uair sheall mi air gach taobh dhiom
Cha'n fhaodainn gun bhi smalanach;
Cha'n fhaicinn coill' no fraoch ann,
'S na daoin' bha leam cha b' aithne dhomh:
Cha'n fhaicinn ach na speuran
Le'n geallach, grian, a's reultan,
A's tonnan borb a' beucail
Air muin a cheil' gu faramach.

Bha sud na chaochladh dhomhsa,
'Bha'n tus mo lo 's na gleannanaibh ;
  Feadh coill', a's fraoich, a's mointich,
Ag arach bho air bhealaichean ;
  'S cha'n fhaicinn muir an uair ud
Gus'n dirinn aird nam fuar-bheann,
  'S cha d' rinn mi urrad's bruadar
Air gabhadh cuain Astraillia.

Gur mor an t-aobhar smaoiutinn
Na daoine caomh bha maille rium,
  Bha uasal, fialaidh, faoillidh,
Gur gann tha aon r'a fhaghail dhiubh ;
  Chaidh iomadh aon gu bas dhiubh,
A's sgapadh cuid 's gach cearn dhiubh,
  'S na tallachan bha blath ac'
Tha 'n diugh 'nan laraich' fhalamh iad.

Ge gealtach roimh na cuantaibh
Na Gaidheil thruagh tha ainniseach,
  Cha mhaireadh ach diombuan iad,
'S bu dualach dhoibh teachd thairis orr' ;
  'S tha iomadh aon 's an uair so
Tha saibhir 's nan daoin' uaisle
  A bha 'sa bhiodh nan truaghain
An Albainn thuath na'm fanadh iad.

Chuinn thu cuid ag radhtuinn
'S na Gasaidean tre aineolas,
  Ri Albainn, tir am mathar,
'N Astraillia 's an Canada ;
  An deigh an reic mar thraillean
Thar chuantan dh' iomal fasaich
  'Chosd bliadhnaibh daorsa 's craidh dhoibh
An saors' o 'maig mu'n d 'cheannaich iad.

Bha Albainn uair mar mhathair
'Bha dilis, blath, a's tairisneach,
  'S cha treigeadh i a h-alach
Fhad 's bhiodh fuil bhlath fo 'h-aisnichean,
  Ach o'n leag Sasunn sail oirr'
Dh' fhas i 'na muime ghraineil—
  Ag altrum clann nan traillean,
A's sliochd nan armunn sgap i iad.

Tha cnid do shaors' an Alb' aig
Fear airgid a bheir barrachd air,
   Ach gann gach tir gu falbh thu
Feadh gharbhlaichean no mhachraichean ;
   Ach oibrich' tha 'na thruaghan,
Le teaghlach lag 's beag duaise,
   Cha 'n eil os ceann nan cuantan
Aon tir a's truaigh' dha fantuinn innt'.

Tha sinn a'm port Dhuneidinn,
'N Otago ann an acarsaid,
   A's chi mi scalladh ceutach,
Air coill' a's sleibh a's gleannanaibh ;
   A's ged nach faic mi sraidean
Le caisteil, 's stiopuill arda,
   Tha coill' a's tir fo bhlath ann
Am bheachds' 'an aill' toirt barrachd orr'.

Thoir soraidh uam 'san uair so
Gu Albainn thuath nam breacanan--
   Gu braithrean 's cairdean suairce
Ri 'n robh e cruaidh leam dealachadh ;
   'S ge mor an t-astar cuain
A ta ead'ruinn air an uair so,
   Mo cheangal riu cha'n fhuasgail
Gus'm bris an uaigh na bannaibh ud.

DR MACRAILD.

Dr Donald Macraild of Greenock was a native of Harlosh, in the parish of Duirinish. The following is a song composed by him on the Island of Skye :—

THOUGHTS ON SGIA, OR THE ISLE OF SKYE.

"Sgeul ri aithris air am o aois."

'S tric mo smaointean onarach.
'S mi 'n seomar dluth air Cluaidh,
Feadh an Eilein cheothoraich,
M'am boidhch' a dh' iadhas cuan ;
Gheobhta fiaghach lan-phailteach
Am monadh ard nan ruadh,
'S chit an t-iasg mar bharcanan
Air traigh nan tonnan fuar.

Theirt' an t-Eilein sgiathach riut
'S cha b' fhiaradh siod air t-ainm,
Rudhaichean is fiaghairdean
Cur fiamh mu t'astar doirbh,
'S lionmhor mu do chriochaibh iad
A' diasganaich 's an stoirm,
Togail onfaidh iarcolta
Bu cholgach riaslach beirm.

Dh' fhaoite nam bu mhiannach leinn,
An ciallachadh na cainnt,
Tir nan lann 's nan *sgiath*-ballach
A ghoirtean dhiot gun taing
'S iomadh laoch dhath d' lionsgaradh,
Na thriall an duchaibh thall,
Dhearbh le sgeith 's le cliaranach
Nach geilleadh siol do bheann.

Bha 'n Teaghlach Tuathach muirneachaibh
'Nad luchairtean air tos.
Eadar Manainn chuirteachail
'S na Tuir a thog na seoid ;
Luingeis chogaidh dluth-bhordach
Bu mhuiseagach fo'n sroil,
'S minic a rinn iad dumhlachadh
Mu Loch an Duin 'sa cheo.

Mheath iad ged a b' uamharrach
An cabhlach luath 's an sloigh,
Ged bha neart a chuain aca,
Mar sin is buaidh tir-mor,
Cha robh sineadh uarach dhaibh
Nuair sheilm an uaigh a coir
'Phasgadh an cuid suaicheantais
An glacaibh fuar an fhoid.

'S beag nach d' shearg na Leodaich uainn
Bu chrodha dol san t-streup.
Dh' fhaodainn chunntadh comhla riu
Clann Domhnuill nan gniomh euchd,
'S Clann Fhionghainn chruadalach
A Strath nam fuar-bheann beur,
Ged dh' uraicheadh dhaibh uachdaran
Dhe'n cinneadh uasal fhein.

Threig Mac Suibhne 'Roag sinn
Bu mhoralaiche geug,
'S Mac Iain Duibh nan cruaidh-lannan
Bho dhualchas nan glac treun,
'S gann gun cluinnear iomradh air
Mur h-ann an iomrall sgeil,
'S Rudhandunain 's Talascuir
Gun tascullach le cheil.

Fearchar Dhunancilirich
'S Niall og bu taght measg leigh,
Peutonaich bu shoilleire
Mar bhoinne 'n gath na grein,
'Fhuair deagh chliu 's gun dhleas iad e
Feadh Bhreatuinn 's ' roinnean cein,
'Dh'fhalbh a h-uile riamhag dhiu
Thoirt riarachadh d'an eug.

C'ait am faighte leth-bhreac dhut
Measg Eileanan na h-Eorp,
Coimeas uidh' us sluaghmhorachd,
Bhiodh suas riut air aon doigh !
'S neamhnaid thu d'ar n-Impireachd
A's fir-ghlaine na 'n t-or,
'S mairidh muirn do shinnsearachd
Gu'n treig bho 'raoin na sloigh.

NEIL MACLEOD.

I need say little or nothing about Neil Macleod. He is
recognised on all hands to be the best living Gaelic poet.
His book, published in 1883, contained 58 Gaelic songs,
and the majority of them have become exceedingly well
known and popular. Mr Macleod is engaged on a second
edition of his songs. The songs which he composed since
that date, some of which have already appeared in the
Highland papers, are to be included. [Note added 21st
March, 1893. The second edition was published in
January, 1893].

"All his productions are characterised by purity of style
and idiom, freshness of conception and gentleness of spirit,
and liquid sweetness of versification. . . . May he

long live to wear his laurels, and continue to delight his
countrymen with new songs of his native land and people."

Four verses are given from Oran na Sean-Mhaighdinn,
because, in the opinion of competent critics, they contain the
best specimen of satirical Gaelic song extant. Most Highland bards tried this line of poetry, but in very many cases
lampoonery was the result. Oran na Sean-Mhaighdinn
can be favourably compared with the best of Horace's
famous satires, written in the Latin language some 1900
years ago. It is full of trenchant wit, without being
offensive :—

ORAN NA SEAN-MHAIGHDINN.

Air Fonn—" Duncan Gray cam' here to woo."

Ma gheibh mise fear gu brath,
Plaigh air nach tigeadh e !
Ged nach can mi sin ri cach,
B' fhearr leam gu'n tigeadh e,
Na mo laidhe 'n so leam fhin—
'S tha e coltach ris gu'm bi ;
Ma tha leannan dhomh 'san tir,
Sgriob air nach tigeadh e !

Ged a bhiodh a sporan gann,
Dhannsainn na'n tigeadh e,
Ged a bhiodh a leth-shuil dall,
M'annsachd na'n tigeadh e ;
Biodh e dubh, no biodh e donn,
Biodh e direach, biodh e cam,
Ma tha casan air 'us ceann
Dhannsainn na'n tigeadh e.

'Nuair a bha mi aotrom og
Phosadh a fichead mi,
Chuir mi dhiom iad dhe mo dheoin,
'S spors dhaibh a nise mi,
Theid iad seachad air mo shroin,
Le 'n cuid chruinneagan air dhorn
Chaill mi tur orra mo choir,
'S leonaidh e nise mi.

Ach ma chuir ird rium an cul,
Smur cha chuir siod orm,
Ach ma 's e 's gu'n tig fear ur,
Sunnt cuiridh siod orm,
Biodh e luath, no biodh e mall,
B' fheaird' an tigh so e bhi ann,
Feithidh mi gu'n tig an t-am,
'S dhannsainn na'n tigeadh e !

MARY MACPHERSON.

In the year 1891 Mary Macpherson *nee* Macdonald
(Mari nighean Iain Bhain) issued a volume of poems and
songs extending to 320 pages. A biographical sketch is
given of the authoress by Alex. Macbain, Inverness, hence
I need not refer to her life here. It would, at anyrate, be
unnecessary, as individual members of the Society know
her well personally by meeting her at some of the Highland
soirees and concerts in Glasgow, many of which she still
attends.

The volume contains 90 pieces of different lengths, on
different subjects, and of different poetic merit.

Eilean a cheo is well-known. It contains 22 verses of
eight lines, the first verse being—

Ged tha mo cheann air liathadh,
Le diachainnean is bron,
Is grian mo leth-chiad bliadhna
A' dol sios fo na neoil ;
Tha m' aigne air an lionadh
Le iarratas ro mhor,
Gu'm faicinn Eilean Sgiathach
Nan siantanan 's a' cheo.

The last verse of this song not only has reference to the
struggles which awakened her poetic spirit into activity,
but expresses the belief that her name and poems would be
remembered by posterity :—

Beannachd leibh, a chairdean,
Anns gach cearn tha fo na neoil,
Gach mac is nighean mathar
A Eilean ard a cheo ;

Is cuimhnichibh sibh Mairi
'N uair bhios i cnamh fo'n fhoid—
'Se na dh-fhuiluig mi de thamailt
A thug mo bhardachd beo.

Mrs Macpherson cannot write her own poetry, but the whole collection, very nearly nine thousand lines, were taken down by Mr John Whyte from the recitation of the poetess. Nine thousand lines of poetry from memory! Her biographer, Mr Macbain, says that she has at least half as much more of her own poetry, and twice as much of floating unpublished poetry, mainly composed by Skye bards, so that she must be able to repeat some 30,000 lines of poetry, 12,000 of her own, and 18,000 of other poets.

LIFE'S WORK.

WHY standst thou idle ?   See, here is thy portion.
Set thy foot firm, let thy furrow be straight,
Haste for thy life, and look not behind thee,
Thy morrow's yoke-fellow rides hard by the gate.

" What," dost thou murmur, " this dreary half acre,
Hard by the common, with weeds overgrown ?
From yon fair field come gay songs and laughter,
Must I then toil in my lot, all alone ?"

Yea, friend, for thou wouldst be greater than other,
Pride and ambition, hold empire within,
Thou wouldst despise thy simple weak brother,
Therefore to thee, is it counted for sin.

Hard is thy lot, but why dost thou murmur ?
Earth opes her treasure-house lavish and free,
Telleth her secrets, and spreadeth her beauty,
Right in thy path, to give glory to thee.

Canst thou not breathe the fresh air of heaven ?
Canst thou not bask in the sunshine of God ?
Canst thou not hear the lark's song of thanksgiving,
Ringing and clear as it mounts from the sod ?

Hast thou not seen the moon in her beauty,
Rise from her couch, 'yond the silvery sea,
Flooding the valley and gilding the mountains,
Fair unto all men, but fairest for thee ?

And hast thou not had thy foretaste of heaven,
Alone, in the hour which awaiteth the dawn,
When silence is felt, and the wings of the angels
Are folded, awaiting the advent of morn ?

Take up thy burden, and cease thy repining ;
Set thy foot firm, let thy furrow be deep ;
" Do with thy might " whate'er thy hand findeth,
That which thou sowest, the angels may reap !

                                              M. O. W.

St. Petersburg.

ON THE IMPORTANCE OF IRISH FOR THE STUDY OF SCOTTISH GAELIC.

By PROFESSOR STRACHAN.

"Antiquam exquirite matrem."

I T is a truism that in order to understand the present form of a language it is necessary to study its past, that to comprehend what a language is, we must know what it has been, and trace out, as far as possible, the various changes which it has undergone, and the different influences which have moulded it during the course of generations. For a practical knowledge of a language this is not necessary. A child reproduces the language of its parents by imitation ; it learns by experience what it may use and what it must avoid, and it may pass through life speaking its tongue with perfect correctness, and at the same time utterly ignorant of the history of the words and forms which are constantly on its lips. So we may learn to speak and write a new language correctly with nothing more than an empirical acquaintance with it ; for this purpose it suffices to know that certain words have certain meanings, and certain forms certain functions, without going on to inquire how these words and forms have come to have their present form and usage. For example, it is enough for practical purposes to know that if you wish to express ' he will do' in Gaelic, we must say ' ni e,' while to express ' he will not do' we say 'cha dean e ;' it is not necessary to know further why in the one case ' ni' is used, in the other 'dean.'

But if we wish also to understand how a language has come to be what it is, how the words and forms have come to have their present form and usage, then we must turn to the historical method. We must trace back the words and forms as far as the written remains of the language will carry us; if necessary, we must call in the aid of cognate dialects and of other languages of the same family, proceeding, as it were, from the twig to the branch, and from the branch to the trunk: it may be that the seeming anomaly of to-day is the result of a law that operated hundreds of years ago. Thus the historical study of Modern English leads back through Middle English to Anglo-Saxon. A comparison of Anglo-Saxon with the other Teutonic languages—Old Saxon, Norse, Gothic, &c. —brings us to the hypothetical proto-Teutonic forms from which have developed, in course of time, the different forms of the individual Teutonic languages. To get beyond this, resort must be had to comparison of these primary Teutonic forms with the corresponding forms of other members of the great Indo-European family—Greek Latin, Celtic, Sanskrit, and the rest. Just as from a comparison of the Teutonic languages among themselves we deduce the original Teutonic forms, so from a comparison of the different branches of the Indo-European family we deduce the original Indo-European forms. Since it is impossible to establish the relationship of the Indo-European family of languages with any of the other languages of the world, the comparative method can go no further. Suppose we wish to trace the history of the word 'three,' cognate with Gaelic 'tri.' Going back to the Anglo-Saxon, we find that the nom. pl. masc. is 'thri.' Comparison of this with Gothic 'threis' and other Teutonic forms, brings us to 'thrir,' as the starting point in Teutonic. Further comparison with the corresponding word in other branches of Indo-European—Lat. 'tres,' Gr. treis, Skr. 'trayas'—leads to 'treyes' as the hypothetical Indo-European form, and nothing more original can be arrived at. Applying the same method theoretically to Scottish Gaelic, we should trace its history back as far as written documents will permit, then call in the sister dialects of

Ireland and Man, and, after arriving at the oldest attainable forms of the Irish branch of Celtic, proceed to compare them with those of the British branch—Welsh, Cornish, and Breton, not neglecting the scanty remains of the language of ancient Gaul, and so get to the oldest Celtic forms. These forms will be the starting-point of comparison with allied forms in the cognate languages. A single instance will shew how important the British dialects may be for the study of Celtic words. The Gaelic and Modern Irish 'og," 'young man,' appears in its oldest historical Irish form as 'oac.' But the Welsh form is 'ieuanc,' and this leads us to 'yovenkos' as the oldest Celtic form, the similarity of which with Latin 'iuvencus' is apparent enough.

But here we propose to confine our attention to the Goidelic or Gaelic branch of Celtic, and here the method, which is theoretically the correct method for the historical study of Scottish Gaelic, turns out to be practically impossible. The reason is that, with one important exception to be mentioned presently, there is no series of ancient documents such as would enable us to trace the history of the language of the Scots after their separation from their brethren of Ireland. Much more is this the case with Manx Ireland, on the other hand, has a literature abundant from he eleventh century, which in the old glosses goes back at least as far as the eighth century, and probably further. Can these documents be used as evidence for the early history of the Highland tongue, or, in other words, was the language of the Scottish Gaels at one time practically identical with the older Irish? The answer, it seems to me, must be in the affirmative. Everyone is aware of the close likeness between the Gaelic of the Highlands and the Gaelic of Ireland, and if we compare not what may be called literary Irish, but the popular dialects, the likeness is still greater. The question may indeed be raised whether the distinction between Scotch and Irish Gaelic is not illusory. What we find is a

4

series of dialects running round the south, west and north of Ireland and the west of Scotland from Waterford to Sutherland, and it may well be doubted whether the differences between the dialects of Argyle and Antrim are greater than the differences between the dialects of Antrim and Kerry. But to answer the question satisfactorily it would be necessary to have a trustworthy account of the various Gaelic dialects of Scotland and Ireland, and unfortunately there seems every likelihood that that will not be undertaken until it is too late. Fortunately we are not left to such vague reasonings from the similarity of the modern dialects of the two countries ; we have a document preserved from the middle ages which shows the practical identity of Scotch with Irish Gaelic at the time when it was written. I refer, of course, to the Book of Deir, from the Abbey of Deer in Buchan.

Let us take a specimen :—Tangator as a aithle sen in cathraig ele 7 doraten ri Columcille si iar fallan (air ba fallan ? Stokes) do rath de, 7 dorodloeg arin mormaer . i . bede gondastabrad do 7 nitharat . 7 rogab mac do galar iar n-ere na glerec 7 robo marb act mad bec . iarsen dochuid in mormaer d' attac na glerec go n-dendaes ernacde lesin mac go n-disad slante do 7 dorat in edbairt doib ua cloic in tiprat gonice chloic pette meic garnait . doronsat in n-ernacde 7 tanic slante do. In modern Gaelic :—Thainig iad an deigh sin gus a' chaithir eile, agus thaitinn i ri Calumcille, oir bha i lan de rath Dhe, agus ghuidh e air a Mhormhaor gu 'n tabhaireadh e dha i, agus cha d' thug e i. Agus an deigh na cleirich a dhiultadh ghabh mac dha galar, agus bha e ach beag marbh. Airsin chaidh am Mormhaor do na cleirich a ghuidhe orra gu'n deanadh iad urnuigh le a mhac, gu'n rachadh slainte dha, agus thug e mar iobairt daibh o chloich an tobair gu ruig cloich Pette mhic Garnaid. Rinn iad an urnuigh agus thainig slainte dha.

The Gaelic of the Book of Deir is practically identical, with Middle Irish, as the following analysis will shew :—

'Tangator,' Old Ir. 'tancatar,' Middle Irish 'tancatar.

tangadar ' (the spelling with ' c ' is historical, ' g ' represents
the actual sound), is the 3 pl. of ' tanic,' he came, Gaelic
' thainig.' The present of the verb is ' ticcim,' I came,
Gael. ' thig.' One of the greatest changes that Scotch
Gaelic has suffered is the decay of its verbal system. The
Book of Deir shews that, at the time when it was written,
Scotch Gaelic, like Irish Gaelic, had not only a much more
elaborate system of tenses, but also different forms to
indicate the different persons of the tense, while in the
modern tongue for the most part the old 3rd sing. is alone
found, with the addition of pronouns to mark the various
persons. Similar decay is found in many of the modern
Irish dialects ; the old verbal system is best preserved in the
dialects of the south.

' As a aithle (sin) ' is a phrase found in Middle Irish in
the sense of ' thereafter.' ' Aithle ' is a noun which seems to
be found only in this phrase ' a aithle,' ' after,' followed by
the genitive.

' In' is the acc. fem form of the article. In modern Gaelic
as in Irish ' an,' pre-tonic ' i ' has become ' a,' as in ' amach,'
Mid. Ir. ' immach ' literally ' in-mach,' ' into the open,' where
' mach ' is the accusative of ' mag,' ' plain ;' the corresponding dative appears in ' amuigh,' Mid. Ir. ' immaig '
' in-maig.'

' Cathraig ' is the acc. sing. of ' cathir,' ' town,' as in Old
and Middle Irish. In the modern language the nom. and
acc have fallen together. The old inflexion in the sing. was
nom. ' cathir,' gen. ' cathrach,' dat. ' cathraig,' acc. ' cathraig.'

' Ele,' Old and Mid. Ir. ' aile,' ' ele,' Mod. Gael ' eile.'
It will be observed that in this extract the rule ' caol ri
caol ' is neglected in writing.

' Doraten ' may be analysed into ' do-ro-aith-tenn,' 3 sg.
pret. of a verb corresponding to Mid. Ir. ' taitnim ' ' to-
aith-tennim,' Gael. ' taitinn,' a verb compounded of ' tennim'
with the prepositions ' to ' (pretonic ' do ') and ' aith '
old Celt. ' .te-' . ' ro ' is the usual prefix of the preterite in
Old Irish, cf. below ' rogab,' ' robo ;' in Middle Irish it

alternates with ' do.' Traces of ' ro' survive in Gaelic in ' robh," ' rug," Mid. Ir. ' ruc,' ' ro-uc ' . . ' ro-uc,' ' rainig,' Old Ir. ' ranic,' ' ro-anic.'

' Ri ' Mid. Ir. ' ri,' ' fri,' Old Ir. ' fri.' In Mod. Ir. it has been ousted by ' le.'

' Si ' = Old Ir. ' si,' Mid. Ir. ' si,' ' i.'

' Iar fallan.' This is evidently corrupt. Mr Stokes suggests ' air ba fallan,' ' for it was full' ; ' air,' Old Ir. ' air,' ' ar ' ' for ;' ' ba,' Old Ir. ' ba,' ' was.' Of ' fallan,' ' full, 'Mr Stokes quotes an example from Mid. Ir. Perhaps the question may be raised whether the correct reading is not rather ' air fa lan ;' ' fa' is a form of ' ba' which is common in the older Gaelic poems, and is also found in Irish.

' Do ' = Old Ir. ' do,' used after adj. of fulness.

' Rath ' = Old Ir. ' rath ' ' gratia,' dat, sg. of neut. noun ' rath.'

' Dorodloeg = do-ro-dloeg, cf. Old Ir. ' tothluchur,' ' I entreat,' ' dotluichethar,' ' exigit,' ' todlaighte,' ' petitum.'

' Ar' seems here to represent Old and Mid. Ir. ' for' after verbs of asking. ' Ar' and ' for' are found confused in Mid. Ir. If this be so, ' forsin ' would have been the Old Ir. form of ' arin.'

' Mor,' Old Ir. ' Mor.'

' Gondastabrad · · Ir. ' con-das-tabrad,' ' tabrad,' 3 sg. sec. pres. of ' do-berim.' ' I give,' ' das' infixed pronoun = ' it.' Such infixed pronouns are very common in Old and Middle Irish ; they have now disappeared.

' Ni tharat.' ' Ni' is the negative particle in Old and Middle Irish, and in many of the modern dialects. Gael. ' cha,' also in some of the Irish dialects, is descended from Mid. Ir. ' nocha,' ' nocho,' ' nochan' ' nochon,' Old Ir. ' nichon,' with loss of the syllable before the accent. ' Nocha' is found in the Dean of Lismore's Book, *e.g.*, Reliquiæ Celticæ, p. 52, l. 15, ' nocha drone' = ' cha d' rinn.' ' Tarat' is the same word as ' dorat' below. The Old and Middle Irish form would also be ' dorat' and ' ni tharat.' The difference of form is due to difference of accent. In verbs compounded with particles, the rule in Old Irish was that, except in the imperative, the accent stood on the second syllable, thus 'dorat,' with weakening of the particle ' to-' to ' do-' before the accent. But after certain particles, of which the negative ' ni' was one, the accent shifted a syllable back-wards, thus ni-tharat (= to-ro-dad-) and as ' to-' here stood in the accented syllable it did not become ' do.' Traces of this double accentuation are still to be found in the Gaelic verbs. Thus ' ni' corresponds to Old Ir. ' dogni,' ' he does,' ' cha dean e' to ' ni dene,' ' he does not.' Similarly ' chi e,' ' chithear e' Old Ir. ' ad-chi' ' ad-chither,' but ' chan faic,' ' am faicear e,' impr. ' faic' Old Ir. ' nicon acci,' ' in accathar,' ' acce (' f' in ' faic,' etc., is a prothetic ' f' already found in Middle Irish) ; ' bheir e' Old Ir. ' do-bheir, ' cha tabhair e ' ' nicon-tabair.'

' Rogab,' ' mac,' ' do,' ' galar,' as in Old and Middle Irish.

' Iarn-,' Old and Middle Irish ' iar n-,' before certain consonants ' iar-,' ' after.' It appears in Gaelic in the infinitive 'tha mi air bualadh.' The form ' ar n-' is already found in Middle Irish.

' Ere,' Mid. Ir. ' era,' ' refusal,' ' craim,' ' I refuse.'

' Na,' Mid. Ir. ' inna-n,' ' na-n,' Old Ir. " inna-n.'

' Glerech,' (c in the Book of Deir here as in ' attac,' ' cloic,' etc., is used to express ' ch') by eclipses for ' clerech,' Mid. Ir. ' clerech,' from Lat. ' clericus.' After a preceding closely connected word originally ending in a nasal, c t p f become in Ir. g d b v, and the medials are assimilated—' an cinn,' ' their heads,' becomes ' a ginn,' now written ' a g-cinn,' ' na m-bo,' ' of the oxen,' is pronounced ' na mo.' There are indications that this change had taken place in Old Irish, though there for the most part it is not expressed in writing. The Book of Deir shows the rule in full force in Scottish Gaelic, in some dialects of which it is said to have survived to the present day. For the most part, however, the original consonants have been restored by a process of levelling. Thus ' na gluas' has become 'nan cluas,' after 'na cluasa,' 'na cluas-aibh,' etc., 'nan' being restored for 'na' from cases like 'nan iasc,' where it was regularly preserved. But the older state of things reveals itself in certain petrified phrases like 'amhan,' 'downwards,' 'down,' doubtless for 'i n-fan,' the preposition 'i-n' = Lat. 'in,' and 'fan,' 'slope.' 'guma,' 'may it be' = 'com-ba'

'Robo,' Mid. Ir. 'robo.'

'Marb,' Ir. 'marb.'

'Act,' *i.e.*, 'acht,' Ir. 'acht.'

'Mad,' Old Mid. Ir. 'mad,' literally 'if it is.' The phrase 'acht mad' is found in Middle Irish, *e.g.*, 'ni ruc claind acht mad oen ingin,' 'she bore no children save one girl.'

'Bec,' Old and Mid. Ir. 'bec.'

'Iarsen,' Mid. Ir. 'iarsin,' 'after that.'

'Dochuid,' Old and Mid. Ir. 'dochoid,' 'dochuaid.'

'Attach,' Mid. Ir. 'attach,' infinitive of 'ateoch,' 'I beseech.'

'Gondendais,' Mid. Ir. 'condentais,' 'dentais,' 3 pl. secondary present of 'denim,' 'I do make,' Gael. 'dean.'

'Ernaicde,' graphic for 'ernaigthe,' or the like, Mid Ir. 'ernaigde,' 'urnaigthe.'

'Gondisad,' 'disad,' by eclipsis for 'tisad = Mid. Ir. 'tisad,' the 3 sg. of the secondary future 'ticcim,' 'I come,' Gaelic 'tig.'

'Slante,' Ir. 'slainte.'

'In edbairt,' literally 'in offering,' 'in,' = Ir. 'in,' 'in ;' 'edbairt,' Old and Mid Ir. 'edbairt,' dative of 'edbart,' 'offering.'

'Ua,' Old Mid. Ir. 'ua,' 'o,' 'from.'

'Cloich,' Ir. 'cloich,' dative of 'cloch,' 'stone.'

'Tiprat,' Mid. Ir. 'tiprat,' genitive of 'tipra,' 'well.' 'Tobar' is the word now in use in Irish as in Gaelic.

'Gonice,' Mid. Ir. 'connice,' 'as far as,' literally, 'till it reaches.' Here it governs the following accusative 'cloich' = Ir. 'cloich.' In modern Gaelic the accusative has fallen together with the nominative. A parallel form in Irish is 'corice' = Gael. 'goruig.'

' Doronsat,' Mid. Ir. ' doronsat' 3 pl. preterite of 'dogniu,' ' I make.'

' Inn,' Ir. ' inn,' accusative of the article ' ind.'

' Tanic,' Ir. ' tanic,' ' came.'

I have analysed this extract at length to show the practical identity of Scotch and Irish Gaelic at the time of the Book of Deir. This identity established, we have at our command for the elucidation of modern Scottish Gaelic, in addition to the scanty fragment of the Book of Deir, the whole range of Old and Middle Irish literature, for, if the Gaelic of the Book of Deir is practically the same as the Irish of its time, its follows that the Old Irish of the seventh and eighth centuries represents a stage through which Scotch Gaelic must have passed, that the language of the Highlands must have had the same fuller system of declension, the same complicated system of verbal forms which we find in the Old Irish glosses. From this it follows that, if we wish to study the history of any Gaelic form, we must, before indulging in any speculation concerning it, first trace it back to its oldest ascertainable Irish form ; except in the few cases where the inscriptions come to our aid, this will be the form found in the Old Irish glosses. It may be that the Old Irish system of inflexion shews either no corresponding form at all or a form from which the modern form cannot, in accordance with known laws of sound change, be derived. In that case, considering the completeness of our knowledge of the Old Irish inflexion system, we may assume with tolerable safety that the form in question is an analogical formation of a later period ; it then remains to search the later literature to discover the starting-point of the new form. A good example of the former type is the so-called Irish consuetudinal present, *e.g.,* ' glanann,' ' he cleanses.' Nothing like this is found in Old Irish, the formation first appears in Middle Irish. It has lately been ingeniously explained as a formation after the analogy of a verb ending in the present in ' an,' inherited from Old Irish. Of the

second type the Gaelic and Modern Irish ' sleibhte,' plural
of ' sliab,' may serve as an example. The Old Irish plural
is ' sleibe.' In ' sleibhte,' which is already found in Middle
Irish, ' te' must have been transferred by analogy from
other nouns where it was the regular form of the plural ;
the particular starting-point future investigation must shew,
for the history of inflexion in later and modern Gaelic has
been little worked at. With regard to vocabulary, it would,
of course, be absurd to apply the same rule. A word
occurring for the first time in the modern language may be
a genuine old Celtic word, which, by some accident, has
not been used in the known literature.

Let it not be supposed that when we have arrived at
the very earliest historical Irish form we have of necessity
reached the goal. It may be that we have ; thus the old
Irish system of accentuation gives a sufficient explanation
of variations like ' ni e,' ' cha dean e.' But we are much
more likely to find that the final explanation is not to be
found in Irish, but that to arrive at it, if it can be attained
at all, we must call in the aid of Comparative Philology,
and search for forms corresponding to the Irish form in the
sister languages of the Indo-Germanic family. In such a
case the tracing back of the word to its earliest historical
form is the necessary preliminary to this further investigation. But to carry this further lies outside the limits of
this paper.

We have already had various instances of the way in
which the older Irish may throw light upon modern
Scottish Gaelic. It may not be without interest to take
some others which have suggested themselves to me while
looking through Stewart's Gaelic grammar. First, as to
orthography. From the fact that certain sounds have
fallen together, for example, ' dh' and ' gh,' and others have
become entirely quiescent, there has resulted much con-
fusion in the spelling of words. Thus is lost the chief
advantage of the historical as contrasted with the phonetic
mode of spelling, that the word bears on its face its past

history. The only way of arriving at the true historical orthography is to trace the word backwards. Stewart has already called attention to this help in fixing the spelling of words. He has been somewhat unfortunate in his examples. As between ' troidh' and ' troigh,' ' foot,' he infers from Welsh ' troedd' that ' troidh' is the correct spelling. Now, the Old Irish word is ' traig,' genitive ' traiged,' and ' g' is found in old Gaulish ' vertragus ;' hence it is evident that the historically correct form is ' traigh.' As to Welsh 'troedd,' it stands for 'troged-,' intervocalic ' g' being lost. Stewart would write ' traidh,' ' shore,' rather than ' traigh,' on account of Welsh ' traeth.' But the older Irish form is ' traig,' and ' traeth' is an entirely different word - Ir. ' tracht.' In modern Gaelic it is customary to write 'thugam,' ' thugad,' ' thuige,' ' to me,' &c., thus altogether obscuring the history of the words. The oldest Irish has ' cuccum,' ' cucut,' ' cuci,' later with aspiration—' chucum,' ' chucut,' ' chuci'—so that the historically correct spelling in Gaelic would be ' chugam,' ' chugad,' ' chuige ;' the words contain the preposition ' co,' ' to.' Stewart, p. 129, distinguishes two prepositions, ' fa,' ' upon,' and ' fuidh,' ' fo,' ' under ;' they both correspond to Old Irish ' fo,' which has both meanings. With regard to ' t'athair,' ' thy father,' Stewart remarks (p. 63, note):—" There seems hardly a sufficient reason for changing the ' d' in this situation into ' t,' as has often been done, as ' t'oglach' for ' d'oglach,' ' thy servant,' &c. The ' d' corresponds sufficiently to the pronunciation, and being the constituent consonant of the pronoun, it ought not to be changed for another." Now, ' t'athir' is found from the Old Irish glosses downwards. As a comparison with Lat. ' tuus' shews, the older form of ' do' was ' to' ; ' to' sank to ' do' because of its weak accent (cf. ' gach' for ' cach,' ' gu' for ' co ;') where, however, the final vowel was elided, the ' t' came to form part of an accented syllable and was preserved, sometimes aspirated ' th'athir.'

We will now take one or two instances from inflexion. In ' ceann,' ' head,' the nom. sing. is the same as the dative. Old Irish had a distinct form for the dative, ' ciunn,' ' ciund ' (= ' cendu'), now ' cenn,' ' cend.' This dative seems to survive in Gaelic in the phrase ' os cionn.' When preceded by the numeral ' da ' the noun has the form of the nom. sing. ' da fhear,' or of the dat. sing. ' da laimh.' This seems very strange, but it becomes clear enough when we turn to the Old Irish declension and find that ' fer ' and ' laim ' are in reality the nom. dual of ' o ' and ' a ' stems respectively. The numerals ' fichead ' and ' ceud ' seem at first sight to take the noun in singular, ' fichead fear,' ' ceud fear.' But when we turn to the older Irish we find that ' fiche' and ' cet ' are substantives governing the genitive case, so that ' fear ' in ' fichead fear ' is not nom. sing., but gen. pl.

' She will bear ' is ' beiridh e,' ' she will not bear,' ' cha bheir i.' There is the same distinction in Old Irish ; after the particle a shorter form of the verb is used ' berid,' ' ni beir.'

On page 68 Stewart treats ' ata ' as a corrupt form of ' ta,' ' tha.' It is the old Irish ' ata,' which is found by the side of ' ta,' which corresponds etymologically to Lat. ' stat,' ' he stands.' ' Ata ' is the same verb compounded with the particle corresponding to the Latin preposition ' ad.'

These examples might easily be increased, but enough has been given to illustrate the principle.

Thus far we have dealt with the outward form of the word. Let us take a couple of instances to show how the older Irish may cast light on the origin and original mean- ing of a word or phrase. Gaelic, like Irish, has a word ' choidhche,' ' for ever.' ' Caidche ' is found in the same sense in Middle Irish, but there are other passages which shew clearly the original meaning ' till night,' ' co aidche.' A good example is found in the story of the sons of Uisnech, Book of Leinster, 260, ' I anatbered immorro in rechtaire chaidche friasi. adfededsi dia celiu inn aidchi sin fachetoir,' ' what the steward said to her till night, she would straightway tell to her husband that night.' ' An deis,' 'after,' probably contains Ir. 'deis,' 'after,' 'each anmain d'eis a cele,' 'one soul after the other,' and this is a nominal preposition containing the word 'eis,' 'footprint.'

With reference to the spoken language our remarks have had more of a theoretical than of a practical interest. We have seen how a study of the older Irish may throw light upon the words and forms of the present day: of the living meaning of the words, and the actual usage of the forms in modern Gaelic it can tell as nothing. The living language must be learned from the mouths of the people. But if we go back to the older Gaelic poems, the knowledge of Irish becomes of practical value. These poems contain words and phrases which have now become obsolete, and which, in consequence, cannot be explained from the living Gaelic language. Here we may not unreasonably expect to get help from the sister language of Ireland with its long literary history. It is with great diffidence that I venture to try to illustrate this, as I am well aware of the danger that one who has to place his trust in dictionaries runs of branding as obsolete a word or phrase still in use. However, the principle is sound, however ill-chosen the illustrations may be. I take one or two examples from the Rev. J. G. Campbell's interesting book, 'The Fianns,' not from any desire to detract from the merits of the work, but to show how a knowledge of Irish may save from mistranslation.

P. 40. 'Marbhar leats' (arsise) caogad ceud' is translated 'There will be slain by thee, she said, nine hundred.' Here 'caogad' is doubtless the Old and Middle Irish 'coica,' 'fifty.' P. 96—

> 'Latha dar dhuinn air bheag sloigh
> Aig Eas Roidh an eiginn mhall.'

Translated—

> 'A day we were but few in number
> At the Red Cataract of the slow-moving fish.'

In Cameron's 'Reliquæ Celticæ' 'Nan eagan mall' of another version of the same poem is rendered 'of the slow-moving salmon.' This word is found in the sense of salmon in Middle Irish. P. 98—

> ' Thainig an laoch bu mhath tlachd
> Le fraoch 's le neart na cheann.'

> ' The hero of comliest form came
> With fury and strength in his head.'

' Inna chend,' ' 'na chend,' is a common Irish phrase for 'towards him.' In the corresponding text in ' Reliquiæ Celticæ,' p. 26, ' nan ceann' is rightly translated ' them to meet.'

One or two examples may be taken from the curious poem ' Am Brat,' ' Reliquiæ Celticæ,' 76, 116. From the affinities of the language of this poem with Irish Gaelic, it is a somewhat exaggerated instance, but it is nothing more than what the student of the older Gaelic literature may have to grapple with. I refer to the version in ' Reliquiæ Celticæ,' 116.

' Fionn as Diarmoid gan on,' ' Fionn and Diarmad without blemish.' ' Cen on' is often found in this sense in Middle Irish, particularly in chevilles—

> ' Mar do ghabh meisge na mna,
> Do bhadar ag iomarbhaidh
> Nach raibhe ar dhroim talmhan tric
> Seisior ban b' chomhaonruic' (read chomhionruic).

' When drunkenness seized the women (a not unknown incident in Middle Irish literature) they fell a-boasting that there were not on the back of the earth six women so honest.'

' Dobhadar,' Mid. Ir. ' dobatar,' ' robatar,' Old Ir. ' robatar,' ' they were.'

' Iomarbhaidh' Mid. Ir. ' immarbag,' ' mutual boasting.' " boasting in rivalry with one another,' ' imm + irbag,' ' gloriatio.'

The precise meaning of ' tric' here is not clear to me.

> ' Cia maith sibhsi as iomdha ben
> Nach derna feis acht le haoinfhear.'

'Though ye are good, there is many a woman that never slept with but one man.'

'Iomdha' is Mod. Gael. 'iomadh,' Mid. Ir. 'imda,' Mod. Ir. 'iomdha.'

'Nach derna' = Gael. 'nach d'rinn,' Mod. Ir. 'nach n-dearna.' 'Feis' serves in Mid. Ir. as the infinitive to 'foaim,' I sleep.' In this sentence 'as' (the relative form) should be 'is.'

> 'Fiafruighes Fionn go n-gaire
> D' inghin an bhrait orshnaithe.'

'Fionn asked with a laugh of the maiden of mantle of thread of gold.'

'Fiafruighes' is the 3 sing. preterite of 'fiafraighim,' the later form of the older Irish 'iarfaigim,' 'I ask.'

'Go n-gaire.' 'Go n' is the Old Irish 'co n' 'with,' a different word from 'co' 'to.' It is found in this poem in 'gon-aille,' 'with beauty.'

'Inghean' is the Irish form corresponding to 'nighean.' Both come from 'inigena,' found on an old inscription. The whole poem abounds in similar instances, but these may suffice as a specimen.

In such investigations it is not sufficient to turn to the native Irish dictionaries like that of O'Reilly. They are full of blunders, and it is unsafe to put much trust in them for the meaning of an obscure word. It is necessary to get a first-hand knowledge of Old and Middle Irish literature, and, thanks to the labours of scholars like Zeuss and Ebel and Stokes and Windisch and Ascoli, that is not difficult nowadays.

Just a word in conclusion on the value of Middle Irish literature for the study of the heroic tales and legends of the Highlands. In the 'Leabhor na h-Uidhre' of the eleventh century, the Book of Leinster of the twelfth century, and later collections, there is a wealth of national story, which should be the common pride of the whole Gaelic race. As time wears on, the older and wilder cycle of legend, that of which the hero is the mighty

Cuchulainn, is thrust more and more into the background (though, as an interesting tale communicated to the Gaelic Society some years ago shows, the memory of the great national epic, the famous ' Tain,' has not completely disappeared from popular tradition), while its place is taken by a new cycle of story, that of Fionn and his followers, who form the chief subject of the heroic ballads of the Highlands. If we wish to observe the growth of these tales, to note what changes they have undergone in the course of centuries, and, if possible, to trace them to their origin, it is to the older literature of Ireland that we have to turn.[1]   And this literature, though it bears the name of Irish, is the inheritance no less of the Gael of Scotland than of his brother of Ireland. It is not meet that prejudice should keep apart members of the same family.   Surely each member of the Gaelic race can be proud of his own tongue without despising that of the others, remembering that they are children of the same mother, and that whatever changes the centuries may have produced, they bear in their lineaments the traces of their common origin :—

" facies non omnibus una,
nec diversa tamen, qualem decet esse sororum."

[1] For an illustration of this principle, the reader may be referred to a discussion of Prof. Zimmer's theory of the origin of the Fionn legend by Mr Alfred Nutt in Waifs and Strays of Celtic tradition, iv., xxi. sqq.   The Irish form of the tale of the sons of Uisneach may be easily studied in the texts published by Prof. Windisch in his Irische Texte Vol. i., p. 67 sqq, and by Dr Whitley Stokes, Irische Texte Vol ii., 109 sqq, who gives an account of other texts of the tale.

HECTOR MACLEAN.

IT is with regret that we record the death of Mr Hector Maclean, the celebrated ethnologist and folklorist. Mr Maclean had completed his 74th year, being born in January, 1818. He was an Islay man, the son of a sailor and skipper. Neil Macalpine, the lexicographer, who, like himself, belonged to Islay, was his first teacher. Maclean, while still a youth, was taken to Islay House as tutor to the younger children, and he accompanied John Campbell of Islay to Edinburgh University as companion and tutor. Here he spent two sessions, working chiefly at chemistry and natural history. Thereafter, he was appointed teacher at Ballygrant School in Islay, an office which he filled till 1872, when, under the new Education Act, he retired upon a small pension.

Mr Maclean first appeared prominently as a Gaelic scholar in connection with John Campbell of Islay's "Popular Tales of the West Highlands." In regard to his share in that work, Professor Mackinnon says :—" It may be said that, while to Mr Campbell is due the credit of originating, mapping out, and publishing the great work, the preparation of no small portion of the material was the task of his able and willing coadjutor." No man of his day was better fitted for the task of editing and preparing such a work. Mr Maclean's *forte*, however, was anthropology. He was an able and keen observer of racial characteristics, whether physical or mental, and his work on Highland ethnology is incorporated in Dr Beddoe's "Races of Britain." He wrote many papers on the early races of Scotland and Ireland ; these have appeared in various transactions and periodicals, notably in the transactions of the *Inverness Gaelic Society* and in those of the *Anthropological Institute.* He had a *penchant* for philology, but in this subject he was unfortunate in his masters, following the guess-work of Hyde Clarke rather than the science of Max Muller. Several of his papers have appeared in our own columns. The only book which he published in his own name was the "Ultonian Ballads," issued last year. We understand that he has left considerable material in MS. form. It is hoped that some, if not all of it, may see the light. A collected edition of his various ethnological studies would form a valuable contribution to the historical literature of the Highlands.

NOTES.

SHERIFF NICOLSON'S poems have been collected and published by Mr David Douglas, of Edinburgh, under the title of "Verses by Alexander Nicolson, LL.D." The editor is the Rev. Dr Walter Smith, who writes a short memoir. The book is neatly got up, and forms a pretty, if not very substantial, souvenir of the genial Sheriff.

THE 44th number of the *Gaelic Journal* has come to hand. In its 16 pages of double-columned quarto, it can comprise a good deal of material ; and the present number is pleasingly diversified with Gaelic and English stories, songs, hymns, proverbs, grammar, and learned notes on dialects and other matters. Some Highland books are reviewed in a series of admirable notes by Professor O'Growney, the learned editor. W. M'K. contributes an old MS. version of the Highland hunting song, " Thogainn Fonn air Lorg an Fheidh."

THE March number of *Folklore* contains an able and exhaustive paper on " Sacred Wells in Wales," by Professor Rhys, a paper that reminds us of the late Alex. Fraser's very excellent contribution on Highland Wells in the Inverness Gaelic Society's Transactions.

A HIGHLAND MEMORY :

Personal Reminiscences of the North, both grave and gay.

BY AN OLD COLONIAL.

With FORTY-FIVE ORIGINAL DRAWINGS and SKETCHES by the Author.

(Specimen Illustration)

IN drawing public attention to this work, the Publishers feel assured that they will earn the thanks of all who appreciate true and delicate humour, frank and generous sentiment, and vivid and accurate portrayal of Scottish character; and they are confident that the book needs only to be known to obtain an extensive and ever-widening circle of admirers and readers. It is elegantly printed, and profusely adorned with vigorous illustrations, full of character and incident, and it is published at a popular price, so as to place it within the reach of all.

PRICE ONE SHILLING

To be had of all Newsagents and Bookstalls, or Post Free, is 2d

"NORTHERN CHRONICLE" OFFICE, INVERNESS

LONDON: SIMPKIN, MARSHALL, HAMILTON, KENT & CO., LTD.

[OVER

Press Notices.

" A capital book for holiday reading. It is light enough to be amusing, is minute enough to be accepted as a broadly-drawn sketch of what actually happens at holiday times in out of the way corners of the West Highlands, and has enough of connected romance in it to maintain the interest of the reader."—*Glasgow Herald.*

" It is a quiet, slowly going, yet always comically satirical account of the everyday life of a remote place in the Western Highlands. The abundance of fun in the book, and its sprinkling of sentiment, are quite enough to palliate any departure from nature in depicting Highland character." —*Scotsman.*

"The author is a Scotchman, and not only can appreciate humour in others, but is somewhat of a humourist himself." —*Manchester Examiner.*

Snould be found in every Scottish household."—*Argus.*

" To the gay, its perusal will enhance the pleasures of a holiday, or compensate for the want of one; and to the grave, will open up views of life, and lines of thought, which they may ponder with advantage."--*The Cateran.*

The Highland Monthly.

VOL. V.

A Magazine which is intended to be a Centre
of Literary Brotherhood for Scoto-Celtic
People both at Home and Abroad.

LIST OF CONTRIBUTORS.

*The following, among others, are to be
Contributors :—*

Lord ARCHIBALD CAMPBELL, Author of "Records
of Argyll."

Sir HENRY COCKBURN MACANDREW, Provost of
Inverness

CHAS. FRASER-MACKINTOSH, Esq., M.P., Author
of "Antiquarian Notes," "Dunachton Past and
Present," "Invernessiana," &c.

Rev. HUGH MACMILLAN, LL.D., D.D., Author of
"Bible Teachings in Nature," "Foot-Notes
from the Page of Nature," &c.

Rev. JAMES CAMERON LEES, D.D., Minister of
St Giles, Edinburgh, Dean of the Thistle and
Chapel Royal.

Rev. DR MASSON, Author of "Vestigia Celtica."

Rev. JAMES ROBERTSON, D.D., Superintendent of
Presbyterian Missions, Manitoba and N.W.T.

JOSEPH ANDERSON, Esq., LL.D., Keeper of the
Museum of Antiquities, Royal Institution, Edinburgh.

A. C. CAMERON, LL.D., Fettercairn.

JOHN MACKINTOSH, Esq., LL.D., Author of the
"History of Civilization in Scotland."

ANDREW J. SYMINGTON, Esq., Glasgow, Editor of
"Wordsworth."

P. J. ANDERSON, Esq., Secretary of the New
Spalding Club, Aberdeen.

Rev. JOHN MACLEAN of Grandtully, Author of
"Breadalbane Place Names."

JAMES CRABB WATT, Esq., Edinburgh, F.S.A.
Scot., Author and Editor of Popular Bio-
graphies.

Rev. JOHN CAMPBELL, Minister of Tiree.

Rev. J. M. MACGREGOR, Minister of Farr, Sutherland.

Rev. JOHN M'RURY, Minister of Snizort, Skye.

Rev. J. SINCLAIR, Minister of Rannoch.

"M. O. W.," Russia.

CHARLES INNES, Esq., Sheriff-Clerk of Ross-shire.

GEORGE MALCOLM, Esq., Invergarry.

ALEX. MACPHERSON, Esq., Solicitor, Kingussie.

WM. MACKAY, Esq., Solicitor, Inverness.

KENNETH MACDONALD, Esq., Town-Clerk of
Inverness.

JOHN CAMPBELL, Esq., Ledaig, Author of Gaelic
Poems

Rev. T. SINTON, Minister of Dores.

T. COCKBURN, Esq., M.A., Royal Academy nver-
ness

CHRISTOPHER T. MICHIE, Esq., Cullen, Author of
"The Practice of Forestry" "The Larch" &c.

No 51.   JUNE 1893.   .   VOL. V.

THE

HIGHLAND

MONTHLY

CONTENTS.

"NORTHERN CHRONICLE" OFFICE, INVERNESS.

EDINBURGH:

JOHN MENZIES & CO.; OLIVER & BOYD; JAMES THIN.

GLASGOW: JOHN MENZIES & CO., AND W. & R. HOLMES.

OBAN: THOMAS BOYD.

CONTENTS

The Highland Monthly.

EDITED BY

DUNCAN CAMPBELL, Editor, "Northern Chronicle,"

AND

ALEXANDER MACBAIN, M.A., F.S.A.Scot

No. 51.   JUNE, 1893.   Vol. V.

FEAR A' GHLINNE.

CAIB. VI.

"GED a bha mi car uine air m' fhaicill air eagal gu 'n
tigeadh na scoladairean ri m' bheatha, chaidh mi
mu dheireadh gu mor as m' fhaireachadh. Ar leam gu 'n
d' fhas iad uile ni bu chaoimhneile rium na bha iad riamh
roimhe. Cha do thuig mi aig an am gur ann air son mo
chur as m' fhaireachadh a bha iad. Ged a bha mi tapaidh
gu leor a dh' fhear m' aoise aig an am, bha mi cho beag go
's nach d' thug mi fa near an cunnart anns an robh mo
bheatha. Gleusta 's mar a bha Naro fhein cha b' urrainn e
a radh co dhiubh a bha gus nach robh mo bheatha ann an
cunnart.

Coma co dhiubh, dh' fhag sinn am baile-puirt gus a
dhol do bhaile-puirt eile, far an robh againn ri pairt de 'n
luchd a chur a mach. Beagan laithean an deigh dhuinn
am baile-puirt so a ruighinn bha sinn air feasgar araidh
'nar suidhe agus 'nar sireadh air ciar-uachdair na luinge a'
cur seachad na h-uine mar is minic a bha ar leithidean
eile. Thainig coltas duine uasail air bord, agus ghabh e
direach far an robh fear dhe na scoladairean agus chuir e
failte chridheil, chaoimhneil air. An ceann tiotaidh chaidh
iad 'nan dithis ceum beag a thaobh, mar gu 'm biodh iad

9

air son diomhaireachd eiginn a leigeil ris do chach a cheile.
O nach robh a h-aon dhinne a bha 'nar suidhe 's nar sineadh
ann an aite eisdeachd cha b' urrainn duinn a dheanamh a
mach ciod e an comhradh a bh' eatorra. An uair a thug
iad greis mhath air comhradh ghabh iad ceum a nall far an
robh sinn, agus labhair an seoladair ruinn mar so :—

"So agaibh, 'fheara, caraid ro dhileas dhomhsa. Is
fhad o 'n a chuir mise 's e fhein eolas air a cheile. Ach tha
iomadh bliadhna o nach fhaca sinn a cheile gus an do
thachair sinn ri' cheile air an t-sraid an latha roimhe. Tha
e caoimhneil mar a bha riamh, agus tha e nis air tighinn a
dh' aon ghnothach le cuireadh do m' ionnsuidh-sa, agus do
bhur n-ionnsuidh-se, gus a dhol air feasgar sam bith a
fhreagras dhuinn gu cuirm a dh' ionnsuidh an taighe aige.
Tha e ag earbsadh ruibh uile gu 'n teid sibh ann. Ged
nach 'eil e eolach oirbh tha e deonach a chaoimhneas a
nochdadh dhuibh uile, o 'n a tha sibh gun chairdean gun
luchd-eolais anns an aite iomallach so."

Thug an duine e-fhein dhuinn cuireadh cho fialaidh 's
cho farsuinn 's a b' urrainn neach sam bith 'iarraidh.
Ghabh sinn uile an deadh thairgse a fhuair sinn. Cha
b' ann a h-uile latha a gheibheamaid tairgse dhe 'n t-seorsa.
Dh' fheumadh gach fear dhinn cead fhaotainn o 'n sgiobair.
Dh' innseadh do 'n sgiobair mar a fhuair sinn an cuireadh,
agus dh' aontaich e gu faigheadh sianar dhinn cead an
tairgse a ghabhail. Bha mi fhein air fear de 'n t-sianar a
thaghadh gus a dhol thun na cuirme. Bha foghail gu leor
orm ris a' ghnothach, cha b' ann idir air son na dh' ithinn
no na dh' olainn, ach o 'n a bha taigh an duine choir beagan
mhiltean a mach as a' bhaile bha toil agam an duthaich
fhaicinn. Ged a bha mi 'nam sheoladair b' e miann
diomhair mo chas a bhith air tir far am faodainn m' aghaidh
a thoirt taobh sam bith a thoilichinn fhein.

Mu dheireadh thainig am feasgar air an robh sinn gus
a dhol thun na cuirme. Nigh is ghlan is chomhdaich sinn
sinn fhein cho math 's a b' urrainn 's a b' aithne dhuinn.
Aig an uair shonraichte bha sinn aig oisinn sraide far an

d' iarradh oirnn an duine coir a thug cuireadh dhuinn a
dh' ionnsuidh a thaighe a choinneachadh. Cha robh sinn
fada 'nar seasamh an uair a thainig da charbad air ar toir.
Chuireadh mise do 'n fhear a bh' air thoiseach comhladh
ris an duine choir a thug cuireadh dhuinn agus ri dithis no
triuir eile nach fhaca mi riamh roimhe. Bha na scoladairean
eile anns a' charbad a bh' air deireadh. Bha am feasgar
air ciaradh anns an am an d' fhalbh sinn.

Ged a bha 'n duthaich mu 'n cuairt oirnn gle bhriagha
cha robh e furasda dhomh fhein co dhiubh beachd a
ghabhail oirre, do bhrigh gu robh an rathad cho dona 's gu
robh eagal orm a' h-uile mionaid gu 'n cuireadh an carbad
car dheth, agus gu rachainn bhar cnaimh na h-amhaich.
Olc 's mar a bha 'n rathad bha sinn a' toirt ceum math as.
Bha mi 'n duil an drasta 's a rithist gu 'n cluinninn na fir a
bha maille rium 's a' charbad ag radh gu robh sinn a'
tarruinn am fagusg do 'n taigh. Ach 's ann a bha iad a'
cath-sheanchus mu mhoran de nithean a chunnaic agus a
chuala iad an uair a bha iad og.

Ann an co-thrath na h-oidhche thainig sinn gu bonn
bruthaich, far an robh coille a bha anabarrach tiugh agus
ard. Ged a chunnaic mise coille far an d' rugadh 's an do
thogadh mi, cha robh innte ach preasarlach beag, bochd an
coimeas ris a choille so. Bha na craobhan neo-chumanta
garbh aig am bun, agus mu dheidhinn na h-airde a bh' annta
cha robh coimeas air. Dheonaich mi a dhol greis a
choiseachd an am dhuinn a bhith 'direadh a' bhruthaich,
ach cha d' aontaich fear seach fear dhe na bha maille rium
gu 'n bu choir dhuinn a dhol a choiseachd idir. Bha
iad ag radh gu'm biomaid aig mullach a bhruthaich
ann an uine ghoirid agus nach b' fhiach e an
t-saothair dhuinn a dhol a choiseachd. Suas
gualann a' bhruthaich bha lub air an rathad, agus chaill
sinn sealladh air a' charbad a bha 'nar deigh. Cha do
ghabh mi ioghnadh sam bith dhe so, oir bha e soilleir
dhomh gu robh na h-eich a bh' againne gu math ni bu
treasa na na h-eich a bh' aig cach. An uair a bha sinn aig

mullach a' bhruthaich chuala siun fead no dha, agus ghrad
leum na fir a bha comhladh rium 's a' charbad air lar.
Thuirt iad gu robh ni eiginn cearr air a' charbad a bha 'nar
deigh, agus gu feumadh iadsan a dhol a thoirt lamh-
chuideachaidh dhaibh. Dh' fhag iad mise nam aonar anns
a' charbad. Ach cha b' fhada gus an d' fhuair mi compan-
aich. Leum dithis de dhaoine dalama, danarra' mach as a'
choille, agus mu 'n do tharr mi scalltuinn ugam no uam
bha iad ri m' thaobh anns a' charbad. Thug an carbad-
fhear suil thar a ghuaille, agus ghrad bhuail e na h-eich,
bha sinn a' cromadh le bruthach, agus bha duil agam an
drasta 's a rithist gu 'm biomaid an coinneamh ar cinn a
mach as a' charbad. Cha bhiodh e ach gann sabhailte
dhomh eirigh 'nam sheasamh, leis mar a bha 'n carbad a'
crathadh 's a' criothnachadh. Agus ged a bhiodh toil agam
labhairt cha b' urrainn dhomh mo bheul fhosgladh. Thuig
mi gu 'n do chuir neach eiginn lion mo mhillidh mu m'
chasan. Cha robh fios agam ciod a theirinn no 'dheanainn
Thainig e fodham uair no dha cruinn leum a ghearradh a
mach as a' charbad ; ach thuirt mi rium fhein gu 'm biodh
e pailt cho math dhomh feitheamh ris a' bhas ge b' e uair
no doigh anns an tigeadh e ri cruinn leum a ghearradh 'na
choinneamh. Cha robh mi idir a' tuigsinn ciod a' bhuann-
achd a dheanadh e do dhuine sam bith mo bheatha 'thoirt
air falbh.

Cha robh an dithis a bha comhladh rium 's a' charbad
a' cur dragha sam bith orm. Ach thug mi an aire gu robh
suil gheur aca orm. Is cinnteach nan d' thug mi ionnsuidh
air teicheadh gu 'm biodh iad 's a' mhionaid air mo thoir.

Mu dheireadh rainig sinn taigh, ach ma rainig, cha robh
tuar no coltas air cuisean gu'm biodh cuirm no fleadhachas
ann an oidhche sin. Chuir a h-uile rud a bh' ann cho mor
troimh a cheile mi 's nach rachadh agam air greim itheadh
ged a bhiodh a h-uile seorsa bidh a b' fhearr na cheile air
a' bhord air mo bheulaobh. Cha b' e coltas taigh duine
uasal a bh' air an taigh idir ; is ann a bha e coltach ri
priosan. Bha greann an uile air gnuis gach neach a bha

mi faicinn. Chuireadh a steach mi do sheomar beag, fuar,
dorcha. An ceann beagan uine thainig fear a steach le
solus agus le biadh do m' ionnsuidh, agus thuirt e rium gu
faodainn gabhail mu thamh uair sam bith a thograinn. An
uair a chaidh e mach as an t-seomar chuala mi e a' cur car
's an iuchair agus 'ga toirt leis as a' ghlais. Sheall mi
mu 'n cuairt orm, ach ma sheall, thuit mo chridhe ann am'
chom an uair a chunnaic mi far an robh mi. Cha robh
aite cadail agam anns an t-seomar a b' fhearr na dha no tri
de bhuird loma. Cha do sheas mi ann an seomar riamh
cho salach ris. Bhiodh naire orm teannadh ris na nithean
a bh' ann ainmeachadh an lathair dhaoine. Bha am biadh
a chuireadh fa m' chomhair air a' bhord, ach cha robh cail
agamsa dha. Cha robh car gorach a rinn mi riamh nach
d' thainig ann an tiotadh fa chomhair m' inntinn. Thug mi
mo mhollachd air an latha 's an d' fhag mi Stocaidh. Ach
an uair a thug mi greis air sileadh nan deur cho frasach ri
leanabh shin mi mi-fhein air an t-seorsa aite-laidhe a bh'
anns an t-seomar, agus dh' fhag mi solus laiste. Mu
dheireadh thuit mi 'nam chadal gu trom.

Cha robh mi fada 'nam chadal an uair a dhuisg mi le
crith 's le eagal nach robh riamh a leithid orm. Ann an
seomar a bha dluth orm bha mi 'cluinntinn gul agus caoidh
a bha 'cur craidh air mo chridhe. Cha b' urrainn dhomh a
dheanamh a mach ciod a bha 'cur nan truaghan gu gul 's
gu caoidh mar a bha iad. Dh' aithnich mi nach b' ann an
trioblaid cuirp a bha iad. Ann am meadhon na caoidh
chuala mi bruidhinn firionnaich anns an t-seomar. Bha e
a' maoidheadh air na mnathan a bha 'gul agus a' caoidh.
Bha e 'labhairt cho fiadhaich 's gu robh eagal orm gu 'n
cuireadh e na creutairean bochda a cochull an cridhe.
Mu 'n d' thainig am feasgar thuig mise gle mhath aobhar
an tuiridh agus am broin.

Gu math moch 's a' mhaduinn thainig an duine dalama,
danarra a ghlas anns an t-seomhar mi a steach gus mo
dhusgadh, agus le biadh do m' ionnnsuidh. Labhair e rium
gu crosd, frithir, an uair a chunnaic e nach do bhlais mi am

biadh a thug e do m' ionnsuidh an oidhche roimhe sin. "Mo
ghille math," ars' esan, "is fhearr dhut do bhiadh a ghabhail
gu math 's gu ro mhath mu 'm fag thu so. Aig an fhortan
tha fios c'uin a gheibh thu an ath bhiadh. Mur gabh thu
do bhiadh an drasta bidh fead-ghoile agad mu 'n d' thig
beul na h-oidhche."

Cha do thuig mi idir aig an am ciod a bha e 'ciallachadh.
Ach dh' aithnich mi air fuaim a ghutha gur e a bha
'bagradh gu garg air na mnathan bochda a bh' anns an
t-seomar a b' fhaisge dhomh' an uair a chaidh e mach as
an t'-seomar chuir e car 's an iuchair mar a rinn e roimhe.

Trom-inntinneach 's mar a bha mi bha beagan dhe n
acras orm. Ach cha b' urrainn dhomh mo bheul a chur
air a' bhiadh a bha fa m' chomhair. Bha eagal orm nach
robh e glan ; agus a bharrachd air sin bha e air a thilgeadh
ugam mar gu 'n tilgteadh gu cu no gu muic e.

An uair a thainig e steach an ceann uine ghoirid sheall
e feuch an do bhean mi de'n bhiadh, agus an uair a
chunnaic e nach do bhlais mi air, spoch e ruin gu fiadhaich,
agus mhaoidh e a dhorn orm, agus thuirt e gu'n d' rinn e
da rud dheug bu mhiosa na h-uile fiacail a bha 'nam
chlaigionn a chur le aon bhuille sios nam shlugaid. Cha
d' fhosgail mi mo bheul ris. Bha eagal mo bhais orm
roimhe. Bha cruth an donais air, ma bha e air duine
riamh. Chuireadh sealladh dhe 'ghnuis oillteil eagal air
dearg mheirleach.

Dh' iarr mi air innseadh dhomh ciod an t-aobhar air son
an robh e 'gam chumail glaiste 's an t-seomar, agus an aite
mo fhreagairt 's ann a thoisich e ri m' bhreabadh 's ri m'
dhornadh. Cha mhor nach do leith-mharbh e mi.

Dh' fhalbh e mach as an t-seomar, agus mu thimchioll
uair a dh' uine thainig e fhein agus burraidh dalama eile,
agus rug iad orm agus cheangail iad mo dha laimh air mo
chulaobh. An uair a thug iad a mach mi ciod a b'
iongantaich leam na gu robh fir is mnathan is clann air a'
cheart diol rium fhein. Cha robh lamhan na cloinne air
an ceangal, ach bha iad, na truaghain bheaga, lapach, gu

bhith air an reic mar thraillean mar a bha mise agus am
parantan. Sin an uair a thuig mise mar a bha cuisean-
Ghrad bhuail e anns an inntinn agam gur e mo reic a rinn
na Seoladairean, feuch am faigheadh iad cuibhteadh 's mi.

Dh' iomaineadh air falbh sinn mar gu 'm biodh treud
dhe na h-ainmhidhean ann. Chaidh sinn troimh
mhonaidhean agus troimh gharbhlaichean ; bha sinn a'
direadh 's a' tearnadh bheann gus an d' thainig am feasgar
anamoch. Theabar ar bathadh uair is uair an am dhuinn
a bhith 'dol thar aimhnichean mora. Ged a bha ar
n-aodach fliuch cha robh doigh sam bith air a thiormachadh
mur tiormaicheadh e umainn. Gun teagamh sam bith bha
'n t-side gle thioram, blath. Is ann a bha i ro bhlath ann
an cridhe a mheadhon-latha. Thainig am feasgar gu bhith
fionnar gu leor, ach cha b' urrainn mi a radh gu robh e
fuar.

Fhuair sinn biadh da uair re an latha. Bha mi fhein
gus mo tholladh leis an acras, agus dh' ith mi na fhuair mi.
Dh' ithinn an corr nan d' fhuair mi e. Thug mi an aire
nach d' ith na mnathan a' bheag sam bith. Cha robh
sunnd itheadh orra, na truaghain.

Anamoch feasgar thaining sinn gu aite anns an robh
coille anabarrach ard agus tiugh. Shuidhich na daoine a
bha 'falbh leinn gu'n cuireamaid seachad an oidhche anns
a' choille, agus gu'n gabhamaid air ar n-aghaidh gu math
moch 's a' mhaduinn an la-iar-na-mhaireach. B' ann mar
so a bha. Dh' fhagadh ceangailte sinn fad na h-oidhche.
Faodaidh neach sam bith a thuigsinn nach robh sinn aon
chuid glan no comhfhurtail anns an t-suidheachadh
thruagh anns an robh sinn. Cheangladh mo dha chois-sa
ri bun craoibhe air eagal gun teichinn, o 'n a bu mhi a
b' oige 's bu luaithe. Cheangladh mar an ceudna gach aon
eile a shaoileadh iad a bhiodh air son teicheadh. O 'n a
bha duil aig na fir ris an d' carbadh ar gleidheadh nach
robh doigh aig a h-aon seach a h-aon dhinn ar teicheadh
chaidil iad gu trom. Cha do smaoinich a h-aon dhiubh
gu 'n tigeadh torachd air duine dhinn.

Cha robh mi 'faotainn bribeadh cadail anns an t-suidh-eachadh anns an robh mi. Bha mo lamhan goirt gu leor, oir bha 'n cord caol, cruaidh a bha 'g an ceangal an deis an craicionn a ghearradh. Ach ma bha mo lamhan goirt, 's ann a bha goirt mo chasan. Air eagal gu 'n teichinn cheangladh mo chasan cho teann 's cho cruaidh ris a' chraoibh 's gur gann a b' urrainn an fhuil ruith annta.

Bha srann aig gach aon mu 'n cuairt orm. Bha eadhon na mnathan bochda a bha cho tursach 's cho bronach fad an latha 's na h-oidhche roimhe sin air tuiteam 'nan cadal. Ged nach robh mise a' faotainn aon bhribeadh cadail, bha mo shuilean druidhte mar bu trice. Uair dhe na h-uairean dh' fhairich mi gluasad am measg an fheoir air an robh mi 'nam laidhe. Thog mi gu grad mo cheann feuch am faicinn an e aon a dh' fhiadh-bheathaichean na coille a bha ann, Ach co a bha 'na chruban ri mo thaobh ach Naro. Stad n da shuil nam cheann, agus dh' fhosgail mo bheul gu labhairt. Ghrad chuir e 'lamh air mo bheul agus chrath e 'cheann. Thuig mi nach robh e air son mi radh aon fhacal air eagal gu 'n duisgeadh an luchd-faire. Gu bog, balbh thug e 'mach sgian as a phocaid agus ghearr e na cuird a bha ceangal mo chasan ris a chraoibh An sin ghearr e an cord a bha 'ceangal mo lamham. Chuir e cagar nam chluais mi 'ga leantuinn. Dh' ealaidh sinn cho failidh ri cat seachad air an aite anns an robh an luchd-faire nan cadal. Gu fortanach cha chuala 's cha d' fhairich iad sinn a' dol seachad orra. An uair a fhuair sinn mu astar ceud slat air falbh uapa, sheas Naro agus thuirt e gu beag rium mi 'ga leantuinn-san a h-uile ceum, agus gu 'n mi radh diog gus an iarradh e fhein orm bruidhinn. A mach a ghabh sinn troimh 'n choille. Tha mi cinnteach gu 'n d' thug sinn co dhiu uair an uaireadair air ruith mu 'n do stad sinn ri failte a chur air a cheile. An uair a rainig sinn iomall na coille shuidh sinn a leigeadh ar n-analach, agus gu cinnte-ach ceart, tha mi 'n duil nach robh mi riamh roimhe no na dheigh cho feumach air m' anail a leigeadh 's a bha mi 'n uair ud. Faodaidh mi radh gu robh mi gun bhiadh gun

deoch gun tamh fad da latha agus da oidhche. Cha robh
sinn fada 'nar suidhe an uair a thoisich an cadal ri tighinn
orm. Ghrad thuig Naro nach robh feum dhuinn suidhe ni
b'fhaide far an robh sinn, o nach robh e 'na aite freagarrach
air son an oidhche a chur seachad ann. Thachair gu robh
beagan de bhiadh aige anns a' mhalaid, agus thug e dhomh
criomag dheth. Cha robh deur uisge ri' fhaicinn, agus ged
a bha am beagan bidh a thug Naro dhomh gu math
b' fhearr leam deoch dhe 'n uisge fhuar na rud sam bith.

Bha againn ri aon cheithir no coig de mhiltean a
choiseachd mu'n ruigeamaid an ath choill. Gu fortanach
b' e fearann briaghа comhnard a bh' ann. Bha preasarlach
coille nach robh ni b' airde na mi fhein an aite 's an aite;
ach b' e feur mor, fada, a bha anns a' chuid bu mho dhe 'n
chomhnard. An uair a bha sinn ma leitheach rathaid thachair
amhainn gun a bhith mor oirnn. An uair a chunnaic
mi i leum mo chridhe leis an toileachadh. Cho luath 's a
bh' agam chrom mi leis a' bhruaich aice a dh'ol dibhe. Bha
mi air thuar mi fhein a mhilleadh ag ol an uisge mur b' e
gu'n do chuir Naro stad orm. Coma leat, 's ann a rinn an
deoch a dh' ol mi feum mor dhomh. Chaidh sinn thar na
h-aimhne gun duiligheadas sam bith. Bha mise deonach
teannadh ri comhradh ri Naro mu thimchioll mar a
thachair dhomh, ach thuirt e rium gu'm b' fhearr dhuinn
cabhag a dheanamh air eagal gu faiceadh neach sam bith
sinn a' dol t oimh 'n chomhnard, agus gu'm biodh uine gu
leor againn gu bhith comhradh an uair a gheibheamaid cuil
bheag air doigh an aite eiginn anns an cuireamaid seachad
an oidhche gu sabhailte.

Mu dheireadh rainig sinn a' choille. Agus an uair a
chaidh sinn beagan air ar n-aghaidh thachair aite oirnn a
bha gle fhreagarrach, ach bha eagal air Naro gu faodadh
daoine a bhiodh a' dol troimh 'n chomhnard solus an teine
againn 'fhaicinn anns an oidhche. Bha mise 'g radh nach
biodh feum againn air teine anns an oidhche idir. Sin an
uair a dh' innis e dhomh gu feumadh teine math mor a
bhith againn air a h-uile oidhche gus eagal a chur air fiadh-
bheathaichean na coille.

Bha mise air fas cho sgith, 's gun ini ach bog, og, 's gu robh mi car coma c'aite an caidlinn. Bha fhios agam nach leigeadh Naro bochd beud do m' ionnsuidh, nam b' urrainn e, ciod sam bith aite anns am bithinn. Air a shou sin bha mi toileach a chomhairle-san a ghabhail anns gach ni.

Chaidh sinn gu math ni b' fhaide steach do 'n choille, agus ciod a b'iongantaiche leinn na gu robh loch boidheach ann am meadhon na coille. Bha e mu cheathramh a' mhile air leud, agus pailt mile air fad. Bha moran de dh' eoin a' snamh air. An uair a chunnaic Naro an lochan bha e an impis a bhith 'dannsa leis an toileachadh. Thuirt e rium gu robh e cinnteach gu robh iasg gu leor air an loch. Ach thuirt mise ris gur beag feum a dheanadh e dhuinn iasg a bhith air an loch 's gun doigh air a thoirt as. Fhreagair e gu robh rud no dha 's a' mhaileid air nach robh fios agam.

Ann an uine ghoirid rainig sinn bord an locha, agus cha robh sinn fada 'coiseachd ris a' chladach an uair a thachair aite ruinn a bha anabarrach freagarrach air son comhnuidh a ghabhail ann. Bha da chreig mhora 'nan seasamh anns a' chladach, agus bha iad mu dheich no dusan troidh o cheile. Cha robh dad againn ri 'dheanamh ach cabair a ghearradh as a' choille agus an cur tarsuinn eadar an da chreig, agus beagan de 'n fheur mhor a bha 'fas an cladach an locha a chur 'na thubhadh air an uachdar.

Thug Naro lamh air a' mhaileid, agus thug e dhomh beagan de 'n bhea an bidh a bh' innte. Thuirt e gu feumteadh an corr dheth a ghleidheadh air eagal gu 'n tachradh dhuinn a bhith latha eiginn gun ghrein a dh' itheamaid. Is gann a bhlais e fhein am biadh idir.

Gun a' bheag de dhail chaidh sinn a ghearradh fiodha do 'n choille. Bha tuadh mhath air so an fheuma aig Naro. Chuir e ioghnadh mor ormsa an tuadh a bhith aige. Thuirt mi ris gu robh a' chuis coltach gur ann a bha duil aige comhnuidh a ghabhail anns a' choille re uine fhada. Cho fhad 's mo bheachd so na ceart bhriathran a labhair e :—

"Beagan an deigh duibh falbh thun na cuirme air an fheasgar ud thachair gu robh mi ann an aite eisdeachd do dhithis no triuir dhe na seoladairean. Thuig mi o na chuala mi dhe 'n chomhradh a bha eatorra nach robh anns a' chuirm a dh' ionnsuidh an robh thusa agus cach air bhur cuireadh ach innleachd a chaidh a shuidheachadh a chum thusa 'reic mar thraill ris na droch dhaoine a tha 'reic 's a' ceannach dhaoine air feadh nan aiteachan so dhe 'n t-saoghal. Air mo chosg bha lan-fhios agam air a' h-uile ni a bha gu tachart dhut. Cha robh mise ach beagan ni bu shine na thu fhein an uair a chaidh mo ghlacadh ann an cearn eile dhe 'n t-saoghal, agus mo thoirt do 'n cheart bhaile-puirt anns am bheil an long an diugh. Dh' fhalbh-adh leam, agus an deigh dhomh fhein agus do na truaghain a bha maille rium a bhith fad cheithir latha air ar n-iomain mar na h-ainmhidhean troimh choilltean agus troimh fhasaichean tiorma, reiceadh sinn mar thraillean air margadh ann am baile-mor araidh. Bha mi coig bliadhna aig an duine eucorach a cheannaich mi mu 'n d' fhuair mi fath air teicheadh. B' e 'cheud ni a rinn e an deigh dha mo cheannach comharradh a chur air cul an t-slinnean agam le iarunn dearg. Tha 'n comharradh sin orm, agus bithidh. Tha mo cheann agus mo chom lan de chomh-arran air na dh' fhuiling mi de dhroch dhiol uaithe fhad 's a bha mi aige. A nis, cha robh fios agam cuin no c'aite am faighinn greim ortsa. Ach bha fhios agam gu feum-ainn biadh, agus gu feumainn teine fhadadh uair is uair, agus mar sin thug mi leam tuadh mhath, paidhear dhagachan, fudar is luaidhe, cuach-theine agus spor agus ascart, dubhain agus driamlach gu iasgach, agus beagan bidh. Mur tig daoine fiadhaich sam bith 'nar rathad cha'n eagal dhuinn ged a bhiomaid anns an aite so gu cionn bliadhna. Mur bi nithean a' dol leinn mar is math leinn bidh ar saorsa againn co dhiu."

Cha robh agamsa ach aontachadh leis anns gach ni. Bha e soilleir dhomh gu robh mi air a bhith air mo reic mar thraill mur b'e gu'n do theisirg e mi.

Cha robh sinn fada 'gearradh na bha dhith oirnn de chabair gus mullach a chur air a' bhothan. Bha Naro a' gearradh agus bha mise' tarruinn nan cabar sios thun a' chladaich. Mu'n d' thainig an oidhche bha bothan beag deas againn anns am faodamaid iomadh bliadhna a chur seachad nan robh doigh againn air gach ni a bhiodh a dhith oirnn 'fhaotainn.

A bharrachd air so bha againn de bhiadh na dh' fhoghnadh dhuinn fad da latha. Cho luath 's a fhuair sinn am bothan ann an scorsa de dhoigh, thuirt Naro g'um bu choir dhuinn a dhol timchioll an locha feuch an deanamaid a mach an robh iasg air. Bha eunlaith gu leor air an loch, agus chuir e ioghnadh oirnn gur ann a bha cuid dhiubh a' tighinn dluth air a' chladach an aite teicheadh air falbh an uair a chunnaic iad sinn. Is docha nach fhaca iad duine riamh riomhe. Thainig sgaoth dhiubh cho dluth dhuinn mu dheireadh 's nach b' urrainn duinn gun teannadh ri caitheamh spitheag orra. Gu fortanach dh' amais sinn a dha dhiubh, agus ghrunnaich Naro a mach gu bann na briogais agus thug e gu tir iad. Thug so misneach anabarrach dhuinn. Dheanadh gach fear dhe na h-eoin ar sath dhuinn le cheile, acrach 's mar a bha sinn. Bha iad gle choitach ri tunnagan, ach bha iad gu math ni bu mho na na tunnagan.

Choisich sinn mu mhile sios ri taobh an locha, agus thachair an amhuinn oirnn a bha 'sileadh as an locha. Mu 'n d' thug sinn ach ceum no dha sios air a bruaich chunnaic sinn gu robh am pailteas de dh' iasg oirre.

O'n a bha am feasgar air ciaradh thill sinn thun a' bhothain. Ann an uine ghoirid bha deadh theine againn air a' chagailte, agus bha fear dhe na h-eoin air a spionadh 's air a dheadh ghlanadh 'ga rostadh air an teine. An uair bha e bruich shuidh sinn aige, agus tha mi 'm barail nach robh mi cho taingeil air son greim a chaidh 'nam cheann riamh roimhe 's a bha mi air son a' bhidh ud.

Chruinnich sinn ultach math am fear dhe 'n fheur a bha fas ann am bord an locha, agus rinn sinn aite cadail a

bha blath, socair gu leor. Bha eagal air Naro gu faodadh
fiadh-bheathaichean tighinn as a' choille air an oidhche
agus ar n-itheadh. Dh' fhadaidh e deadh theine ann an
dorus a' bhothain, leig e leamsa dhol a chadal an toiseach,
agus dh' fhan e fhein 'na dhusgadh gus an do thoisich an
latha ri soilleireachadh.

R'I LEANTUINN

SIR THOMAS URQUHART OF CROMARTY.

BY ALISTER DAVIDSON.

PART II.

AFTER the execution of Charles First, Sir Thomas Urquhart joined the Mackenzies of Pluscarden, the Munros of Lumlair, and others, who rose in arms; placing themselves at the head of their respective followers, they possessed themselves of the garrison of Inverness, and planted the standard of Charles Second in that town. For his part in this rising, Sir Thomas was proclaimed a rebel and a traitor by the Estates of Parliament at Edinburgh on the 2nd of March, 1649. Having cast in his lot with the Royalists, he seemed determined to see the struggle fought out to the bitter end; and, in 1651, we finding him lodging in the house of one Mr Spilsbury, in the town of Worcester. After the disastrous Battle of Worcester he was taken prisoner. But a far greater disaster befel him, for the soldiers of Cromwell raided the house of Mr Spilsbury, and took possession of seven "portmantles" in which Sir Thomas had stored manuscripts in folio "to the quantity of six score and eight quires and a half, divided into six hundred and forty and two quinternions, the quinternion consisting of five sheets and the quire of five-and-twenty." The great bulk of his beloved manuscripts he never recovered, but one quinternion had the fortune to fall into the hands of "a man of some learning," who returned it. Another complete work was rescued from the flames by Captain Goodwin, an officer of Colonel Pride's regiment.

The lot of Sir Thomas Urquhart, as a prisoner of war, was hard. He was confined for a considerable time in the Tower; and it was only after long negotiations, and the

personal intervention of Cromwell, that he was released
from prison on parole. His financial situation, and his
general prospects in life, were in a desperate condition;
his creditors had taken possession of his estates, and all
hope of a successful career in the service of the State was
gone for ever. Most men would have yielded to the
situation, by abandoning their Royalist principles and making submission to the Commonwealth; but Sir Thomas hit
upon an expedient which few men could have invented or
dared to put into execution. He asked from Government
his release and the return of the Cromarty estates, free from
burdens incurred by his father, basing his claim on three
grounds:—First—The antiquity of the Urquhart Family.
Second—The wisdom and learning of the head of the
family, shewn by the invention of a universal language.
Third—The prospect of future inventions which would
greatly enrich the country. In support of his claim he
published a series of works unparalleled in literature for
their eccentricity and extravagant verbosity. He set forth
the past glories of his family and his own merits in bom-
bastic and inflated periods, which might well move to envy
the prospectus writer of the present day. It is impossible
to compare the style in which these works are written with
that of any other known writer. The author invents and
distorts words at will; he lays every language known to
him under contribution, and he delights to build up huge
polysyllabic words, which are absolutely meaningless; yet,
notwithstanding his extraordinary literary method, he tells
us that he affected "the purity of the latine diction."

In *The Promptuary of Time* he traces "the true pedigree
and lineal descent of the most ancient and honourable
name of the Urquharts in the House of Cromarty, since
the creation of the world until this present year of God,
1652." He opens his extravagant genealogical work with
the creation of Adam. "God the Father, Son, and Holy
Ghost, who were from all Eternity, did, in time of nothing,
create red earth; of red earth framed Adam, and of a rib

out of the side of Adam fashioned Eve. After which
creation, plasmation and formation, succeedeth the generations as followeth." The earlier portion of the Urquhart
Family history is apparently drawn from the genealogies
given in the earlier Books of the Old Testament. Passing
over centuries, we find, among the more distinguished of
the clan, Esormon, Sovereign Prince of Achaia ; Zeron,
agnamed Bacchus, whose castle and lands were forfeited by
Eugenius Octavus, King of Scotland, because of his
hospitality to Donald of the Isles ; Vocompos, who, for
valour, received back the lands of Urquhart from King
Solvatius. To this chief the Urquharts owe their crest, for
we are told that " Vocompos was the first in the world that
had the bear's head to his arms ;" he being induced to
adopt this crest by King Solvatius, because of his great feat
of slaying three bears in the Caledonian Forest. Sir Jasper
Urquhart had the power of curing king's evil by the touch
of his hand ; he was, for his valour, " dubbed knight by
Malcolm Kiaenmore at Forfar in the yeer of our Lord,
1058." The Urquharts seem to have had a happy faculty
of marrying into good families. An early Urquhart
married a niece of Findok, King of Scotland ; another
married a daughter of Nectanus, King of the Picts ; and it
was the good fortune of a later member of the clan to
marry a daughter of Rodrigo, Captain of the Morrays, and
first Morray that ever came to Scotland.

In 1653, Sir Thomas published " An introduction to the
Universal Language.' The work was dedicated " to all
pregnant and ingenious spirits." The author announces,
that having applied himself to every branch of human
learning, and, having " mastered what was already known,
and finding the amount but little," he had resolved to add
to it ; accordingly, he sets before his readers a scheme of
Universal Language. He appears not to have been the
only seeker after a Universal Language, for in *Burnet's Life
of Bishop Bedell* it is related that in 1633 a certain clergy-
man, named Johnston, " of mercurial wit," proposed to lay

before the Bishop a plan for resolving all languages into one. In 1773, Lord Monboddo gave it as his opinion that Greek was the only perfect language, and it ought to be used by all ; and, in recent years, we have had, at least, one serious proposal for the adoption of a Universal Language. Sir Thomas Urquhart proposed, by the use of the associative faculty, and by an elaborate system of classification, to reduce language to a system, starting from a fixed root or base. His alphabet consisted of six vowels and twenty-five consonants. Simple ideas were mono-syllables, and every added syllable expressed an idea. To use the author's own words, some of the advantages of the language were—" Every word in this language signifieth as well backward as forward, and however you invert the letters still shall you fall upon significant words." . . . " In framing of rime, the well versed in that language shall have so little labour, that for every word therein he shall be able to furnish, at least, five hundred several monosyllables of the same ter-mination with it." . . . " In the denomination of the fixed stars it affordeth the most significant way imaginary ; for by the simple word alone which represents the star you shall know the magnitude together with the longitude and latitude both in degrees and minutes." . . . " This language will be so convenient that if a general, according to the rules thereof, will give new names to his soldiers, whether horse, foot, or dragoons, as the French used to do their infantry by their *noms de guerre*, he shall be able, at the first hearing of the word that represents the name of the soldier, to know of what brigade, regiment, troop, company, squadron or division, he is, and whether he be of the cavalry or of the foot, a single soldier, or an officer, or belonging to the artillery or baggage " . . . " The greatest wonder of all is that of all languages in the world it is the easiest to learn, a boy of ten years old being able to attain to the knowledge thereof in three months space."

10

It has been said that this scheme of a universal language was an attempt to carry out the maxim—

" You'd best begin with truth, and when you've lost your
Labour there's a sure market for imposture."

But there can be no reasonable doubt that the author's belief in the feasibility of his plan was sincere, for he shows by his observations that he had considered the subject deeply and had spent time and pains upon it. It is, however, impossible to accept the scheme in a serious light, it must be placed with the discoveries of men of extravagant imagination and sanguine temperament, who search wildly and eagerly for the impossible and unknowable, and after a time become firm believers in the reality of an imaginary discovery. The pains and labour spent in devising this scheme may not have been wholly thrown away, for imaginary discoveries and false theories sometimes do lead to the truth, and as the author says— " In an hypothesis it is not always the theory itself which is to be regarded, but oftentimes the sparks and scintillations which irregularly fly off from it."

Much information as to the universal language is to be found in another work by Sir Thomas, published in 1652. "Eskubalauron ; or the discovery of a most exquisite jewel, more precious than diamonds inchased in gold, the like whereof was never seen in any age ; found in the kennel of Worcester streets the day after the fight and six before the autumnal equinox, anno 1651. Serving in this place to frontal a vindication of the honour of Scotland from that infamy whereinto the rigid Presbyterian party of that nation, out of their covetousness and ambition, most dissembledly hath involved it " The scope of the work was " to entreat the honourable Parliament of this Commonwealth, with consent of the council of State thereof, to grant to Sir Thomas Urquhart of Cromarty his former liberty, and the enjoyment of his own inheritance, with all the immunities and priviledges thereto belonging." The book opens with an extravagant account of the merits of the

universal language, it then discusses some of the reasons
why the Scottish people were looked upon with disfavour,
and it winds up with an account of some eminent natives of
Scotland, and, in particular, the adventures of the Admirable
Crichtoun. The curse of Scotland is asserted to be the grasp-
ing propensities of the Presbyterian clergy. "How this
covetousness, under the mask of religion, took such a deep
root in that land, was one way occasioned by some
ministers, who, to augment their stipends and cram their
bags full of money, thought fit to possess the minds of the
people with a strong opinion of their sanctity, and implicite
obedience to their injunctions; to which effect, most
rigidly Israelitizing it in their snynagogical Sanhedrims
and officially bragging in their pulpits, even when Scotland,
by divers notorious calamities of both sword, plague, and
famine was brought very lowe, that no nation, for being
likest to the Jews of any other, was so glorious as it."
The clergy, he assures us, hypocritically counterfeit
devotion, "the better at last to cast anchor of profit, which
is the but they aimed at, and sole period of all their dis-
simulations." He cherished a singular hatred to the
Presbyterian clergy, and he never loses an opportunity of
savagely attacking them. His whole attitude to the clergy
of Scotland reminds us of the saying of a celebrated French
statesman—" La Cléricalisme, voila l'ennemi."

Of Sir Thomas Urquhart's translation of "Rabelais," it
is now needless to speak. It is Hall-marked by the
approval of three centuries, and it may be regarded as one
of the most perfect transfusions of an author from 'one
language to another, that ever man accomplished."

There is some authority for saying that Sir Thomas
Urquhart is the author of a singular production—*A Century of Names and Scantlings of Inventions*. The book
is generally attributed to the Marquis of Worcester: it
contains a catalogue of outlines of inventions, some of them
bearing a striking resemblance to inventions claimed by
Sir Thomas in his books. It is probable that the apparent

resemblance is the only reason for attributing the book to him.

While Sir Thomas Urquhart was striving, by the influence of his works, to obtain a complete pardon from Parliament, he was released on parole; and, after a time, he was allowed to go for five months to Scotland to look into his affairs. He found that his creditors, believing him to be dead, had taken possession of his estates. So enraged were they at his re-appearance that they used influence with the Government to have his parole recalled. At length they succeeded in making his position so precarious, that he returned to London, and once more he was re-committed to the Tower. Apparently the only bright memory he had of his visit to Cromarty, was the kindness of William Robertson of Kindeasse, "for his going contrary to that stream of wickedness, which carried headlong his fellow-creditors to the black sea of un-Christian dealing."

The remaining days of the Knight of Cromarty are wrapped in mystery. It is said, that escaping from the Tower, he fled to the Continent; and that he died in a fit of excessive laughter on being informed by his servant that Charles the Second had been restored to the Throne.

Such, in meagre outline, is the story of Sir Thomas Urquhart's life. It is to be regretted that we have no material for pursuing a further enquiry into his career. If he had seen fit to leave an autobiography, there cannot be a doubt that it would have proved a literary curiosity, which would have charmed and delighted future generations.

It is difficult to form any precise or definite opinion as to the character of the man. Among literary men of any era he would have been regarded as singular; and in the age in which he lived his career must have been looked upon as eccentric in the extreme.

He was an idealist, striving to attain a perfect combination of the soldier, the man of the world, and the scholar. His ambition was to maintain what the Germans call, "a life of heart and mind," while, at the same time, taking an active part in the political life of his time.

He delighted in regarding himself as a man of principle, attaining his ends by fair means, without resort to political chicanery. Speaking of himself in the third person, he says :—" I dare swear, with a safe conscience, that he never coveted the goods of any, nor is desirous of any more, in matter of worldly means, than the peaceable possession of what is properly his own ; he never put his hand to any kind of oath, nor thinks fit to tie his conscience to the implicit injunctions of any ecclesiastical tyranny. He never violated trust, always kept his parole, accounted no crime more detestable than the breach of faith. He informs us that he never received a bribe, played the hypocrite, or flattered a superior, and he proudly declares that the enemy never saw his back except on the field of Worcester. He sums up his confession of faith with the assurance that the main ground of all his proceedings is honesty." There is no reason to doubt that his moral character was of the highest description. What we know of his public life is greatly to his credit. To his political straightforwardness and honesty he testified with his body, and although, perhaps, in his writings his veracity is not above suspicion, his statements are the highly-coloured exaggerations of a visionnaire and a dreamer rather than the deliberate falsehoods of an impostor.

His failings were many, but they were the amiable weaknesses of harmless personal vanity rather than those of selfish egotism. His vanity and conceit are apparent in every page of his books. In the frontispiece he is depicted seated on Parnassus surrounded by the Muses, and he does not fail in the preface to assure his readers that they are about to wander in a literary garden, adorned with the most luxuriant flowers of rhetoric and imagination.

John Stuart Mill has defined genius "as the gift of seeing truths at a greater depth than the world can penetrate." It was the fixed belief of Sir Thomas

Urquhart that he possessed this quality in the very highest degree -the Almighty having given to him alone the power to pry out and discover the secrets of nature.

In the story of his life, we cannot fail to admire the courage and stout heart with which, when overwhelmed with misfortune, he faced the world. Poverty, imprisonment, and the persecution of his creditors failed to break his spirit or damp his literary ardour. He sounds a triumphant note when he says of fortune—

" Nor hath she any chaine wherewith to bind
The inclination of a noble mind."

He possessed culture, learning, and considerable inventive talent, but his books are burdened with tiresome pedantry and pompous diction, relieved only from monotony by his extravagant drollery and wonderful capacity for collecting and heaping up extraordinary epithets. If his works are not entitled to a very high place in literature, they, at least, merit perusal as the writings of a " prince among pedants,' whose curious humour and absurd intermixture of ingenuity and exaggerated folly cannot fail to amuse us. He united the characteristics of the pedant, the humourist, the inventor, the soldier, the patriot, and the courtier ; a combination so amazingly incongruous that he deserves to be remembered as one of the most singular literary characters known to history.

A STRANGE REVENGE.

By D. Nairne.

CHAPTER XX.

FLORA'S MESSAGE.

'THE artist of the parish, old Willie Fraser, was busy
chisel and mallet in hand, evolving from a large slab
of freestone a suitable graveyard memorial to the laird.
With David's consent, the schoolmaster had already
brought his literary skill to bear upon the construction of a
suitable inscription. It had been read in the smithy, and
approved by a majority in that final court of appeal. The
minority, of whom Willie was one, objected to the dominie's
Latin, not because it was not good enough in its way, but
on the ground that if—and it was unanimously admitted—
the deceased was "a man of men and a laird of lairds," the
public should have the benefit of the statement in plain
English. Whether—

> " Vir Virorum
> Dominus dominorum"

should or should not be inserted on the stone, became quite
a public question, the discussion of which reached a climax
when the minister one Sunday indicated his opinion of the
controversy by a sermon on the duty of being simple to the
simple, even in the matter of kirkyard legends. However,
the schoolmaster's pedantry gained the day. He rolled the
phrase on his tongue like a sweet morsel ; it formed the
groundwork of several lessons to his advanced pupils ; it
became the stock complement of the smithy ; the plough-
man chanted the ponderous syllables in the fields, the herd
to his kine ; the whole community were, in fact, seized with
the rhythm of the couplet as with an epidemic. Between

this and a neighbouring parish there was an old-standing feud ; but now, it was averred, the clinching argument had been reached—" We hae better Latin in oor kirkyard." All of which is only worthy of mention because of a certain conversation it gave rise to on the particular day we find it of interest to make the said Willie Fraser's acquaintance.

Willie paused in his labours now and again, rubbed his stubbly chin—for it was on the eve of his weekly shave—and gazed meditatively across country. It was apparent that he had, as the colloquialism went, " something on his mind."

" The hale thing's hankle queer," he declared audibly after an unusually prolonged pause, " I dinna think I'll haud my tongue longer aboot it. Had that feckless body's ' vir virlorums' no driven folk clean daft mair than I might hae put twa and twa thegether afore noo."

After this summing up, he resumed the beat of the chisel, but presently the lazy rattle of approaching wheels made him pause.

" That's farmer Simpson back frae Inverness," he informed himself ; " a decent chield is Tammas, and the very man tae crack over the subject wi' ; sae the laird will jist wait half an hoor langer for his stane."

" It's takin' shape," shouted the new comer, as he brought horse and cart to a stand-still.

" No sae fast as I would like ; but, ye see, its the best bit sandstane I've put chisel tae, an' the workmanship must be correspondin'. "

" I wudna care aboot yer job—gey soberin' tae the thochts, I reckon, wi' the emblems o' death aye afore yer een."

" There are mair mysteries than the mysteries o' death," was Willie's answer, as he drew forth pipe and tobacco, " the mysteries o' life are mair puzzlin' than those o' death. Every ane is bound tae discover the latter for himsel' sometime or ither, and so he needna trouble himsel' ; but the mysteries o' life may gang on forever."

" Yer richt—completely and unequivocally richt, as the minister wad say ; for, man, Willie, things happen that makes ye rub yer e'en an' speir if ye were no dreamin'."

" Talk aboot the mysteries o' Latin, there's a guid sicht mair that's queer up at the Castle there, if I'm no mistaen, than the mysteries o' a' the dominorum's—the schulemaister's capable o' inventin'."

" Weel, seein' that you, a man o' sense, as we a' consider ye, gie that opinion, I dinna mind tellin' ye, straught, its my ain tae. As certain am I as I'm sittin' on this cart, I saw Maister Richard ridin' pell mell intae Inverness in the middle o' the nicht—the nicht after the laird deed. I had been spendin' an oor wi' Farbairn, an' had a gless or two in my head, I admit, but it would tak a wheen mair o' them to cheat me that it wusna the laird's mare an' Richard Stewart on her back."

" Tuts, tuts, I'm afraid ye had mair whisky than ye mind o'—Maister Richard was then lyin' sick in Edinbro. There's nae disputin' that fact. If ye saw onything ava it must hae been his ghaist—speerits seem to be walkin' the earth unco common in thae times."

" Ghaists when they gallop dinna fill yer een wi' stoor ; nor dae they put up their horses at coach hooses, an' tak tickets tae Edinbro wi' the mail, as was done in this case. The groom that took in the mare is as certain as he's alive that the rider was Maister Richard in disguise."

" In disguise !"

" That's the wonderful thing—in disguise."

" Weel, that's even queerer than what I saw mysel'—an' I've telt naebudy aboot it. On the very nicht the laird deed and Miss Flora recovered, I walked round the hoose, no bein' able tae sleep, like, an' wha did I see come runnin' oot o' the Castle grunds but the witch, mutterin' an' tearin' her hair ! That was the last that was seen o' the puir woman in this world. Since then I've learned—though John and the ither servant folks are keepin' their mouths shut aboot it—that the witch was in the Castle that very nicht, an' had something tae dae wi' Miss Flora's recovery —wha kens, but wi' the laird's death, tae? She was never done cursin' the puir man."

"Puttin' a' thing together, it seems tae me there's something sadly wantin' clearin' up," pronounced Farmer Simpson. "The whole Castle appears tae have gaen tae the deevil a' at ance."

"Whist, man, that's no the way tae speak ; no, no, I wudna say that ; but I would venture this—as my private opinion—that Professor Somerton, who made a moonlicht flittin', has a hand in the pie somehow ; an' what you mention aboot Maister Richard confirms that impression. However, things are dreadfully mixed up, an' had better be let alane in the meantime. Truth, like murder, will oot ye ken."

The conversation was here prematurely interrupted by the appearance of John, who was walking quicker than usual, and looked brimful of news. It was to the effect that the body of Elspeth, the witch, had been found floating down the river, and that though considerably decomposed, there was nothing on the body to shew that death had been due to violence.

"It's strange, John, ye should step upon the news the very minute we were discussin' aboot the poor creature," remarked Simpson.

"I could tell ye things mair strange than that," was John's reply : but as he shewed no disposition to do so, Farmer Simpson, with a knowing wink of the far off eye, gave "gee-up" to his horse, and Willie resumed his chisel with a solemn shake of the head, while John, apprehending from the demeanour of both that he had been indiscreet, also departed in silence.

From that moment rumour became busier than ever in the district, its favourite shape being that Richard had refused to marry Flora, had quarrelled desperately with his father, who died from excitement (if not actually from violence), and that Richard, in disguise, had flown to a strange country to join the Professor and his daughter. David, pursuing as he now did, the habits of a recluse, was ignorant of these stories, but, as it accidentally transpired, they had a marked effect in the part of the drama he had chosen to play.

The laird's death, coupled with Richard's absence, his reputed illness, and, above all, his mysterious silence, were retarding influences to a woman of Flora's temperament, but she soon recovered from her prostration and resumed her duties in the household. She had now lost, however, every shred of her natural gaiety. Hers was a mechanical activity. From no one was it possible to conceal –least of all from David—that she was sad and unhappy. In the circumstances, her situation was a cruel one, for there was not a human being in the world to whom she could confide her trouble and obtain sympathy and advice. Knowing as she did David's feeling towards her, even the consolation of his company she as much as possible avoided.

There was another unhappy being in the Castle, and that was David himself. He had chosen the thorny path, and did not find it easy going, though in every particular fortune had favoured the successful execution of his plans. He was beset with fears of discovery, of revelations that might destroy for ever the hope he entertained, once Richard's character had been explained, as he intended to explain it, of winning Flora's hand. So far he had not dared upon any statement beyond what was contained in a business letter from the family solicitor in Edinburgh—that Richard was ill, and that he had been imperatively ordered upon a long sea voyage, which was to have America as its termination in the first instance.

"But why does Richard not write to me?" Flora asked in tremulous voice.

Here was an opportunity, almost an invitation, to explain the whole situation of affairs, but David shrank from it, and remained silent –and his silence, and apparent agitation, suggested to Flora fresh fears ; either Richard had deserted her, or (and she clung rather to this alternative) he was too ill to fulfil the promise he made to write her ; what if he, too, were dead !

" For Heaven's sake," she implored, " tell me all, David ; I know you are concealing something from me which I am entitled to know—is Richard ill, I mean very ill ?"

" The last letter I had from our Edinburgh agents stated quite the reverse. He had called upon the firm, and was on the eve of entering upon a sea voyage. You must remember, Flora, that Richard has not written me a single line any more than you—but I don't complain, of course, of his silence, except for your sake."

Without another word Flora left the apartment ; for there only remained the heart paining question of Richard's faithfulness, and with that, she told herself, not even his brother had concern. In its consideration she did not have recourse to tears ; hers was a love even above chiding. The conclusion at which she arrived came naturally and spontaneously in her simple, womanly philosophy of the matter—if Richard had really left her, then must he have found greater happiness elsewhere ; and as all she desired was his happiness she must be content. She must not complain, only suffer, for in herself lay the blame, surely, of not being able to retain his heart in exchange for her own.

This conviction brought with it a sense of chastened tranquility, and as the weeks passed it settled down upon her as if it had been the decree of years. She again began to move about amongst the people, resuming those little philanthropic attentions to the aged and the infirm which had endeared her so much to the community around. It was but natural that, ere many days passed, the gossip of the countryside should reach her ears ; insinuatingly, and in sympathetic comments at first ; and then, as she innocently probed the thing to the bottom, the full force of the scandal, and the mystery of it, faced her with paralysing force.

Thus it was that David had forced upon him the dreaded interview at which he had resolved to expose

Richard's conduct in its worst possible light, and thus lay the foundation of what, he fondly hoped, would ultimately lead to the fruition of his own love dream. Surely, he argued, a woman who had been deserted and wronged in the manner Flora had been would, however deep her love, turn round and spurn the man who had done it? He argued, it will be seen, upon the general and accepted sense of the character of female nature, and the ordinary principles of human action ; and he omitted, as the majority do, that great mystery in affairs of the heart, the "love that loves alway," regardless of consequences and events.

When David entered the room, in response to her summons, Flora rose—pale, nervous, yet resolute-looking—and confronted him with an enquiring gaze, the meaning of which he had no difficulty in interpreting. What had she learned? For the extent of her information he was not quite prepared : it upset all his carefully arranged story, and threw him back, in his extremity, upon a bare state-ment of facts. In other words, her first question saved him from himself ; for one deliberate falsehood, which he had planned to tell if necessary, requires a sliding scale of other lies in its support, generally bigger—if there be such a thing as comparatives in untruths—than the original ; and the scale may slide on for a lifetime.

"David," she said, "I have some questions to ask you, and I beg—on your honour—that you will answer me truthfully. I told you before that I had an impression there were some things you were hiding from me which I ought to know. The first inkling of their nature you have left the villagers to give me. Even the servants refuse to say anything, and refer me to you, so I am sure there must be something dreadful to tell. Did Richard come back from Edinburgh and go away again, when I was ill, and father was dead—did you know of it, David, for they say so outside? Say they must be mistaken—I told them so—that it is impossible."

Tears were stealing down her cheeks as she concluded ; and she drew herself up with a gesture of surprise as she noticed the effect her words had upon David, whose face had become ashen. He had not intended to tell of the secret visit—it would be more damaging, he had convinced himself, to represent Richard as having run off, regardless of the consequences of his actions; but as Richard evidently had been seen, to make a clean breast of it was, he felt, the only course left to him.

"Yes, Flora, I will tell you the whole truth—and, believe me, if I have kept back anything, it has been from a desire not to give you pain."

"What care I for pain now," broke in Flora, "tell me everything, let it be ever so cruel, and I will bear it."

"Then Richard did come back, Flora; but we agreed that nobody should know of it—for certain reasons which are not pleasant ones, either for you or anybody else."

"I think I can—guess them," said Flora faintly, and resuming her seat, "is that all?" She could not bear to be told in plain words that Richard had deserted her, though her heart knew it, and felt sore; and that was the only statement she thought David's words could imply.

"That is not all, Flora; unhappily, it is far from all. You were ill; would you believe it, that Richard was the cause—I mean the voluntary cause—of that illness, which might have sent you to your grave—which made it possible for you to have been buried alive?"

"David," cried Flora, starting up, "you promised me to tell the truth; do you deliberately ask me to believe *that* of Richard; do you believe it of your own brother?"

"Flora, I am telling you the truth, and you must not doubt me like that. I must believe what I say, seeing I had it from his own lips, and on the written evidence of another party to his guilt."

She stood with hands clenched to her bosom, and stared into David's face as if for confirmation of the thought that the whole story was a fabrication; but now that he felt the ground firm beneath his feet, his manner forbade even a suspicion of that nature.

"I cannot comprehend," she said, almost in a whisper.

"It is a strange story, Flora ; but let me first explain, in justice to my brother, that he did not anticipate the awful consequences I have described. In that he was innocent."

"Whatever Richard did," said Flora, softly, "I will never believe that he intended to injure, far less kill me— but this is all so queer, that I seem to be dreaming, as I dreamt during that illness. I seemed then to be in the world and yet not of it ; is this another delusion?"

"It is the reality this time, the cruel reality ; and a stranger chapter in family history has not been written."

"You say Richard caused my illness; tell me how and for what motive ; quick, for this is maddening!"

"Forgive me if I put the matter in plain words, Flora."

"Yes, tell me the worst, the absolute worst."

"He wished, then, by a certain physical treatment, to make you cease to love him."

A smile of relief and incredulity stole over Flora's face, and she scrutinised David for an explanation which had suddenly occurred to her—was he mad?

"Are you dreaming, David, or are you mocking me?'

"I am doing neither, Flora, I am but telling you actual facts, which, as I remarked, make up an exceedingly strange story of a man's wickedness. If you sit down, I will detail to you everything, and you will be more astounded even than you are now. It also involves, as you will see, my poor father's death."

"Father's death ! You told me the cause of his death already."

"Yes, but the shock was given by a certain letter, which contained a terrible revelation—one which was, fortunately, untrue as regards yourself, for you are alive, and not murdered, as was represented, by Richard. That statement killed him."

"I get more and more mystified, yet it seems as if the Witch's curse were all coming true."

And that scene in the hut, after she saved Elspeth's life,

flashed upon her—the prediction, too, that she never would be mistress of the Castle.

" It was the Witch who saved your life, Flora—wicked as she was (she evidently had some hand in the plot), she did you a good turn before leaving the world. Sit down, please, and bear what I have to tell you as bravely as you can."

Flora mechanically obeyed, and as brief as possible, with perhaps a slight tendency to exaggeration when he touched upon the part Richard had played in what he not unhappily called the ruin of their house, David narrated all that had occurred—the Professor's extraordinary plot of revenge ; Richard's gullability ; the escape Flora herself had made through a quickening of the Witch's conscience ; and he dwelt upon what he knew Flora recognised as the outstanding feature of the whole matter, his desire that she should love him no longer, in order that he might, with an easier conscience, enjoy the affections of another woman. Yes, he guessed correctly, that was the uppermost, the humiliating thought, in Flora's mind, and she could see no way in which the fact could be minimised—innocent though his intentions had been—that besides the desire to get rid of her love, the foolish means which he had adopted to gain that end had imperilled her life. Well, having regard to herself, better it would have been had she slept unto death, she told herself ; then, no, she argued, it would have made Richard unhappy ; had David not just stated that he was repentant and miserable?

" Yes," reiterated David, " he seemed to be crushed under the weight of his guilt. If any man was repentant for a foolish and dangerous action, it was he."

" Yet, though you told him I was alive, which should have made him happier, he went away without a word, and without asking my forgiveness," commented Flora, assuming, what David had been careful not to touch upon, that his brother would necessarily have hastened to the relief of Richard with the assurances of his victim's safety.

"Would he have been forgiven?" asked Richard, showing surprise in his tone.

"The greatest sinner may be forgiven," she sighed, "and in the committal of this sin he has not been the greatest to blame."

"But he wanted to lose your love, Flora," Richard contended, feeling that he had the whiphand of the argument, and that it would be to his advantage to press home that primary view of Richard's conduct.

Flora saw it, and did not reply for a time.

"You say he repented," she remarked at last.

"What human being would not repent in similar circumstances?"

This, both felt, brought the conversation to a natural conclusion, and yet both knew that, in their respective interests, something more required to be said. Flora, supporting her head with one hand, gazed sadly, wistfully, at the tapestry, wondering whether Richard's professed repentance might not imply more than David imputed to it—escape from the consequences of his misdeed; might it not mean that he again loved her? On his part, David was debating within himself whether it would be advisable for him to declare his love there and then, and thus give her thoughts a new and healthier turn. That she should continue to love his brother was a possibility he could not conceive.

"Flora," he at last mustered up courage to say, "my brother has wronged you very grievously. However you may continue to regard him, I, at anyrate, cannot longer consider him worthy of your love. I am ashamed of the weak part he has played; it is sad to think, is it not, that through his foolishness our home has been rendered desolate by death, and everyone made miserable. You are unhappy, and have cause to be, for has he not given you the greatest humiliation it is in man's power to inflict upon woman? Try and forget him, Flora, as he forgot you and his duty towards you. After a time, when things have mellowed down, you may again be happy. Fate, try to think, has decreed that things should be as they have happened. There is some one still left to love you, and whose love will never change. You already know that I love you tenderly. If you cannot by-and-bye return my love, at least think kindly of me, as one who would verily lay down his life to be of service to you, if it would secure your happiness—and do not avoid my company, Flora, dear, as you have done these many months past. It has made me miserable. Surely a man's love, though your own heart may be elsewhere, deserves more consideration. Will you not allow me, Flora, to make up by my devotion for the injury Richard has done you ? I do not ask it now, but may I not hope some day to have your sympathy, and hear you say that you appreciate my love ?"

While speaking thus in a quiet voice of entreaty, David had taken Flora's hand, and she allowed it to lie listlessly within his. But unresisting as she was, he knew it was not yet dawning time for even the hope that she would give him encouragement to win her heart. She sat motionless, with a far-away look, unmoved by his words, and apparently feeling no interest in them. He dropped her hand, and it fell by her side—a silent but eloquent dismissal which he accepted with a sigh. Presently she roused herself, and there was a kindlier ring about her voice which partly dispelled the gloom which had begun to settle upon him, while her proposal stirred him by its unexpectedness.

" You said Richard had gone to seek revenge, and that bad health was but an excuse for his absence. He may commit a great sin, in inflicting that for which there is no need, and which is very wrong. We have suffered through this Professor's wickedness, but his suffering physically will not assuage our grief. As his brother, have you not thought that it rested upon you to prevent him bringing harm to himself and to others ? You have said it would give you pleasure to be of service to me."

" I would do anything, Flora, for your sake, anything ;" but he did not suspect the sacrifice she was about to demand.

" Then leave at once and bring Richard back ; it may even yet not be too late."

" Are you serious ?"

" It is your duty as his brother."

" And if he will not come back, Flora, which I fear is all too probable—he was so ashamed of himself?"

" Then leave my message with him—that I forgive and still love him."

" That, Flora, after all that has happened ?"

" After all that has happened he stands in need of my love more than ever. Poor unhappy Richard," she added, half in whisper.

" Should he refuse to come home ?"

" You are going, then ?"

" Your desire is my command, and I shall deliver your message faithfully, if I can find him."

" That is kind of you, David, but you must consider that you are only doing your duty."

" And after it is done, Flora ?"

" Come back to me."

With these enigmatical words she left him. What a difference there is between what the imagination conjures up as bound to occur and what actually happens ? An interview like this, and with such a result, he had never in the remotest degree anticipated. He had pictured Flora grief stricken and upbraiding, and she was forgiving and loving ; he had imagined her protesting that she never wished to see Richard's face again, and she despatched him to bring him back. The more he thought of it, the more he disliked the mission ; for what explanation that would approach the real truth could he give Richard for concealing from him the fact of Flora's recovery? And the consequences? That night he felt decidedly uncomfortable and more than half regretted the unreserved offer of service he had made to Flora, consuming as was his passion for that unhappy individual.

CHAPTER XXI.

THE UNEXPECTED AGAIN HAPPENS.

"WHAT is your impression to-day, doctor, as to her chances of recovery?"

"Her bodily health continues to improve, which is a hopeful sign, and for a brief space yesterday I thought I detected a glimpse of returning intelligence in her manner. Ten to one, her reason will return as suddenly as it left her. She is marvellously pretty. Providence will surely be kind to spare such a noble specimen of womanhood from the blight of a life-long disordered intellect."

"May God grant it so."

The speakers were Richard Stewart and Dr Halliburton; the latter the owner of a private establishment in the outskirts of New York. After the deathbed scene in prison, Richard had obeyed the dictates of humanity, and made it his first duty to see after the welfare of the Professor's unhappy daughter. He found that she had absolutely no friends, and that the only refuge open to her was the public asylum, where she would be received as a common pauper. The outcome of a medical consultation was the assurance that Julia's case was by no means hopeless, and he accordingly at once placed her under the care of the most distinguished expert in the States in mental diseases. At Dr Halliburton's he was a frequent visitor, and gradually the doctor had drawn from him the story which had had so tragic a denouement. But beyond taking this humane interest in Julia's welfare, Richard had formed no plans for the future. He found life in New York new and interesting, and for the present he was content to allow things to drift. Into the stir and social vortex of the busy city, he, by his friend the Doctor's advice, threw himself as much as possible to drown the agony of that other tragedy by which, as he supposed, Flora had been sent to a premature grave. Once his quest for revenge ended, remorse had seized him in such violent paroxysms that his coming in contact with Dr Halliburton was, in a measure, fortunate for himself.

" Unless you resist this grief which you naturally feel," said the doctor kindly, " I will have two patients to cure instead of one. You acted innocently—in fact, with damnable innocence—and though you deserve to suffer, there is no necessity for your becoming mad."

Another subject gave Dr Halliburton—thoughtful, kind-hearted fellow as he was—some concern, and that was the relationship which the two young people would assume towards each other when Julia recovered. As matters were going he could foresee only one result, and that was marriage, but he argued that the alliance of two people of such temperaments, each of whom would recall to the other a sad episode in their lives, could scarcely be either happy or healthy. Accordingly he one day broached the question in an indirect way to Richard, on grounds which he was well aware were a little fallacious.

" Mr Stuart," he said gravely, " Miss Julia is improving rapidly, so rapidly, indeed, that when she saw you from the window yesterday she appeared startled, and asked who you were. I am afraid the sudden discovery of your identity might give her a shock which would have unpleasant consequences. Would it be too much to ask you to stay away till I again summon you hither ? "

The keen eyes of the doctor at once detected, though Richard promptly agreed to banish himself, that he was keenly disappointed. He refrained from putting the case plainer in the meantime, but had Richard been able to read what was in the doctor's mind at that moment, he would have departed much gloomier than he felt. Though she was removed from him as it were by a gulf, these daily visits to Julia were a source of infinite pleasure to him, and their cessation, temporary as he believed it would be, filled him with something like dismay. As he walked towards his hotel that evening, the world seemed to him blacker than it had ever appeared before ; little did he dream that he was on the eve of an event which would give the cloud that overshadowed him a silver lining.

"A gentleman wishes to see you, sir," was the announcement made by the waiter an hour later.

"Shew him in," said Richard wearily, but the next instant he had leaped to his feet, and was staring with unbelieving eyes at the gentleman who had entered the room.

"Am I dreaming, or is it the phantom of my brother?"

"No, Richard, it is your brother in the flesh."

"But why have you come?"

"Must you know that before you even shake hands?"

"Pardon me, but you know suspicion haunts the guilty mind, and I feel criminal. Heartily glad am I to see you, though such an undreamt-of pleasure is suspicious of evil tidings."

"Let me say at once, that my news is good, but that to me personally my mission is by no means pleasant. Richard, you little suspect that I have done you a great injury, and hope its reparation is not too late. Have you seen the Professor?"

"I did see him—before he died."

"You did not kill him—for God's sake tell me."

"I was going to, but death, with his own help, cheated me of the pleasure ; which I do not now regret."

"Thank heaven for that."

"Why? You are raising my curiosity to an enormous pitch. What is your sin?"

"Flora recovered, and I hid the news from you."

At the words Richard staggered back and clutched the mantelpiece for support.

"I do not know what possessed me that night, but somehow I had the notion that you ought to be punished for your folly," David went on to say, with downcast eyes, for the humiliation of his position stung him severely. "Perhaps, also, a selfish motive was at the bottom of it. It was mad of me. Can you forgive, Richard? Only now does the serious nature of my conduct come fully home to me. I see it all—and what might have been the terrible consequences of my behaviour."

"Flora is alive?"

"Alive and well when I left home to find you.'

"And she was alive when I was with you in your room, torn with the agony of remorse, the very epitome of misery and degradation?'

"Yes."

"You allowed me to leave my home, though my father's dead body lay there—or is he, too, alive and well?"

"No."

"And you call that conduct brotherly? David, I never expected such treatment at your hands; wretched as my conduct had been, I did not deserve it. You mention consequences; it is the merest chance that you do not find me a murderer in reality. Think of that! You ask forgiveness, but I hesitate, David, I really hesitate."

After a while, when David had delivered Flora's message—which, needless to say, greatly moved Richard—and made a clean breast of his feelings towards Flora, they got on more friendly terms, and proceeded to discuss the situation in a practical aspect, though the question of forgiveness was not again touched upon by either.

"I must think over the matter for a night," said Richard, referring to Flora, "and in the morning I will consult Dr Halliburton before giving you my answer whether or not I shall return to Scotland."

The Doctor looked much amazed when he found Richard in his study next morning, but when he heard the news his feelings were evidently those of profound gratification.

"You ask my advice, sir; well then, Julia knows you are here and longs to see you. Judging from your conduct you do not really love this girl Flora. So you will stay and make her your wife, go up country and farm, and live a sunny life ever after. The news that Flora is safe and

that you still love her will make Julia as sane a girl as there
is in New York."

A few weeks later, the two brothers stood hand in hand
on board a ship, the anchor of which was being weighed
prior to her departure for the mother country.

" I hope you may win Flora and make her very happy
—God bless you both," was Richard's parting remark ; and
all David could do was to return the hand pressure.

CHAPTER XXII.

THE END.

THE sun is setting over a flourishing American homestead
—flourishing in golden grain, mostly in stook ; in fat kine
which low at the gates ; in the powerful teams which have
already, during a few days' lull, begun to haul the winter
logs ; in the general activity round about, and in the trim
order which everywhere prevails—for slovenliness has
always spelled ruin in capital letters, anyhow in the long
run, as Richard correctly argued in the practical light
which had developed in his character.

" Come, Julia, I want you out to see the sunset ; it is
our seventh anniversary, you know, and I promised you a
walk."

" Shall I take the children, Richard ?"

" Not to-night, love—you understand ?"

And she understood.

They halted near a giant pine, and without a word their
arms wound themselves about each other.

" Have the years seemed long, darling—seven long
years ?"

They have passed like a dream, Richard—at this rate
life will be far too short."

" You have no regrets ?"

" Absolutely none ; and you ?"

" Only one."

" Oh, Richard, what is it ?"

" That I cannot live those seven years over again."

" Richard."

" Yes."

" Let us in our happiness remember Flora."

" We will write to her to-night, and make her little namesake sign the letter—won't it be a surprise for her ?"

That letter, with its childish signature, speeds on its way to the gloomy old castle—gloomier now with its unkempt ivy obscuring the windows, and the untended grass half hiding each shrub. The paternal acres have been sold, and among the new tenants is John, who makes an excellent farmer, albeit the reddest in the countryside, while his sonsy wife Kirsty has not lost a single pound of flesh, though in her own words, she " fechts fra mornin' till e'en tae mak' ends meet."

The occupants of the Castle are two in number— Flora Macgruther, spinster, and David Stuart, bachelor. They occupy separate wings of the building, and seldom meet. David, they say, has become queer in his habits inasmuch as he seldom ventures out of doors except under cover of night, when he occasionally startles a stray pedestrian by silently traversing the broad acres which his ancestors tilled for so many generations. They say he stays indoors in case he should meet Flora, who continues to devote herself to philanthropic work in the parish, others that he is preparing a *magnum opus* (that is the school-master's phrase) on medicine ; but perhaps John's is a more correct version than any, that he has been driven " queer in the head." However that may be, certain it is that one night he was heard to remark—for he had lately fallen into the habit of keeping up a continual babble to himself when he fancies he is alone—" Ha, ha ! it *was* a strange revenge !"

[CONCLUSION.]

LETTERS CONCERNING SIMON LORD LOVAT AND HIS AFFAIRS. 1701.

BY MR FRASER-MACKINTOSH.

WHILE there are hundreds of letters extant after Lord Lovat's return to Scotland in 1715, few are known in connection with the obscure part of his history from 1696 to 1702. The three letters after given, written early in 1701, are of special interest, as showing how heartily a really good man, Sir Hugh Campbell of Calder, took up Lord Lovat's cause and believed in his innocence of the charges so maliciously made and ruthlessly followed up by the Athole family. The letters were written a few days prior to the Justiciary trial, nominally at Lady Lovat's instance, and it seems evident that Lord Lovat, and friends like Calder, were confident of acquittal. William III. favoured Lovat, and were it not for the King's death, and the immediate re-accession to power of Athole under Queen Anne, Lord Lovat need never have been an exile.

The first letter is from Calder to David Ross of Balnagown, whose mother was Mary, daughter of Hugh Lord Lovat and Isabella Wemyss, and Lovat and Balnagown were thus first cousins. Again, Calder and Balnagown were married to sisters.

"Calder, 30th January, 1701.

"Right honoured,—It was yesterday morning my Lord Lovat left this, and I doubt not but he will be with you ere now. He has my Lord Argyle's letter anent him to me, which he will shew you, but I send this express without any man's knowledge or desire to tell you that it will be greatly for your honour to assist and support my Lord Lovat at this time, and it will gall and grieve that (once great) man who attempted to affront you (if not more) opened the mouths of very many to the prejudice of his own honour. If I hade not put my son in fee of my estate, or if it had pleased God that himself had lived, I would readily have advanced as much money as would buy my Lord Elcho's comprising, and I hope you will do so, which will be as honourable an action as ever I knew performed, with so much money, nor can you lose a sixpence of it, for my Lord Lovat will be content if you keep the head for the washing. The worst that can follow upon it is that it will disappoint and displace some certain self-interested persons, who if they do not hate have little kindness for you or him, which will be sufficiently counterbalanced, and much more than so, by the honour which will accress to you by supporting a person of so much merit, and so considerable a family in whom you are so much concerned, and to whom you are so many ways related ; and for whose preservation you so lately and so publicly expressed your zeal. So that I am very hopeful, all things considered, you will see it fit to do all that is in your power for my Lord Lovat, which I am weel informed will do all that he has to do, and I am sure it will make you beloved in this generation by all good men that hear tell of it, and posterity for many ages will remember so great and so good an action to your honour, and will embalm your name better than all the apothecaries ointment would do your body, and preserve your memory better than any marble or ivory tomb would do. This will be like a new founding of the family, and there is no Lord Lovat that will ever come but will be curious to see how his rights are founded, which they cannot do but they must at the same time see what you shall do for them, and so I pray God direct you, and I give my humble duty to my Lady, and being in some haste, and hoping or indeed I assure myself of a good answer, I remain, sir, your affectionate brother to love and serve you,

(Signed " H. C. of Calder.

" To the Laird of Balnagown."

The second letter is addressed to the Earl, afterwards Duke of Argyle, and is creditable to Calder as kinsman and clansman of the great house of Campbell. The Lovat lands of Kirkhill are those referred to, as then holding of Argyle. It is likely that one or other of the letters would have had the desired effect, had it not been that all negotiations fell through in consequence of Lovat's involuntary withdrawal.

" Calder, 30 January, 1701.

" Right Honourable,—The design of my last letter was
that your Lordship might endeavour to get some more time
for the raising of money to buy that comprising of my Lord
Elcho's which is so absolutely necessary, and upon getting
of which my Lord Lovat's recovery seems to me to depend
so much that it is a sine qua non. But this letter is to
shew your Lordship that without more time its next to
impossible for my Lord Lovat himself to raise the money,
and though he could, as I still fear he cannot, in so short a
time. That which I am for, is that which I projected and
intended when I first wrote to your Lordship, which is that
your Lordship would please to raise the money on your
own credit and take the right of Elcho's comprising in your
own name, and then dispone Lovat and a considerable part
of the estate to this Lord and his heirs male to be holden
of the King, and dispone that which he has already holden
ward of your Lordship, to be holden as he had it formerly,
and to dispone the rest of the estate to him to be holden in
feu of your Lordship and your heirs with the burden of a
feu duty equivalent to the annual rent of the money you
will advance or near it, and by this means you will fix and
secure their following, not only for this debt which I hope
you have done already, while this Lord Lovat lives, but for
all time coming for holding a part of his lands ward and
paying to your Lordship a considerable feu duty will put
the family ever under a necessity to depend upon your
Lordship, and will put everybody else from attempting for
a conquest of that estate when they see they must hold it
of your Lordship on such terms. Perhaps your Lordship
may think this is no good advise because it will increase
your debt, but I hope it may be far otherwise and it will
cost your Lordship no more but the trouble of once raising
the money in the first instance, for I make no doubt but
your Lordship may raise it from your friends in the shire of
Argyle by way of a volunteer stent, and he is no true
Campbell who will not be willing to pay his proportion of
any stent which may be requisite for so honourable and
great an occasion, which at once raises the interest and
honour of your Lordship's family upon which the well being
of your kinsmen does so much depend that they must stand
or fall with it, as they have seen evident by what happened
to the family within this 40 years. How were they trod

upon when your grandfather was in trouble? What could they call their own after the death of your father till it pleased God your Lordship was restored to your right? so that I may say that any Campbell that will not contribute what is in his power to the preserving, advancing, and raising of the interest and honour of your Lordship's family is unwise with respect to his own preservation as well as unnatural and ungrate, for its certain when the tree is cut down the branches must fall and wither. And that your Lordship may see that what I say is in sinceritie, my own opinion shall be my practice, and I will take care that my interest shall do as much and more, for I think this as honourable an occasion for your asking and your friends granting a supply as ever happened in my time. So my Lord I pray you miss it not and make yourself master of that comprising of Elcho's as I have said, and I doubt not that you will recover the money in this method, and so without expense or loss, or anything that can be blamed in your conduct, make a very great addition to the interest and honour of your family.

"I spoke to my Lord Lovat himself of this design when I wrote first to your Lordship of him before my Lady Lovat was carried south. I put him in mind of it yesterday before he left this, and I find him very willing to have it so, but told me withal that it was that which he would do to no other man living but yourself, to whom he acknowledges he owes his life and fortune next under God and the King, and so I intreat your Lordship, and I doubt not but you will be active in this matter of Elcho's, for all depends upon that comprising. The design of this letter is so important and so expressive of my affection and duty to your Lordship and family, and my zeal for preserving, advancing, and raising your honour and interest that I hope it will procure your Lordships pardon for the length of it, and so I pray God bless and preserve you and your family and make you more and more capable to advance the public good of Church and State, and that you may be ever under His special care and protection, I wish with all my heart, who am, right honoured, your Lordship's most faithful and humblest servant,

Signed   "H. C. of Calder"

"To the Earl of Argyle."

The last letter is forcibly put, and the hearty acknowledgments of all Frasers are due to Sir Hugh Campbell for
his description of them as " a numerous clan of the prettiest
men, and most addicted to arms and virtue and frugality of
any people in the Northern Highlands."

" Calder, 7 February, 1701

" Right Honoured and my Noble Lord,—Having had
the honour to be acquainted with both your grandfathers,
to whom I was much obliged, and specially to the Earl of
Wemyss his favour upon several occasions, and of being
my lord your father's utmost comarade, who treated me
with all the familiarities and respect that could be betwixt
brothers, and what I am to say being what can never prejudice you in point of interest, but will tend much to your
advantage in point of honour and will oblige very many
persons who are both capable and will be ready to serve
you. I cannot fear that your Lordship, who carries so great
a character, can be displeased with what I am to propose,
the granting of which will not only confirm the good
opinion and esteem, but raise the hopes which the virtuous
part of mankind, to whom you are known or who have
heard of your name, have conceived of you.

My Lord, I am informed that your Lordship has the
first comprising against the Estate of Lovat, and the present
Lord Lovat being your Lordship's near cousin, I am glad
that its in your power to preserve him and his family, which
is indeed very ancient and noble, and commands a numerous clan of the prettiest men and most addicted to arms
and to virtue and frugality of any people in our northern
Highlands. I am likewise told that albeit others purposing
to suppress this present Lord Lovat has been dealing with
your Lordship, and would have bought the comprising, but
that your Lordship was pleased to order your trustees that
my Lord Lovat himself be preferred to the buying of it at
the price of 20,000 merks. He has been in this country
speaking with his friends from whom he was to raise it, and
has done more than could be expected in so short a time.
He is greatly beloved as any man that ever I knew, and if
he could have stayed but a fortnight or 20 days longer in
his own country he would certainly have got all the money

raised and your Lordship satisfied, but being obliged for
his own vindication of a crime whereof his virtue made him
incapable to go south and appear before the Justice Court,
and having raised Letters of Exculpation for eliding a
caluminous sic libel upon reasons and grounds so relevant
as can admit of no dispute, which he is able to prove by
many honest witnesses and gentlemen of honour whose
integrity is beyond exception. He was forced to lay aside
his more private affairs till it were over, which makes it
necessary for him to have, and I hope will move your Lordship to grant him, some more time to provide your money,
which I am confident your Lordship may be as sure of at
Whitsunday, and I hope sooner, as if it were already
in the bank. I shall use but few words to persuade
your Lordship to grant this which I will take
as a very great favour, and first that he has the
honour to be your Lordship's near cousin. Next
the getting this comprising will certainly restore him and
preserve his family, and the putting of it in any other hands
will as certainly ruin him, and the preserving him will lay
an obligation upon him and his friends, who are very many,
and all that come after him, of love and honour to your
Lordship and your noble family, and make him capable to
serve you and to pay that duty and respect to which you
have so just a claim by his being befriended of you, which
must be raised to the greatest height by your supporting
and preserving him at this time from inevitable ruin ; and
there is no man of honour but must approve and commend
your lordship for your preserving your near cousin and his
ancient noble family from ruin when it can be done so
easily, as the delaying the payment of that money for some
short time. My Lord, I begin encourage myself to hope
as if you had already granted it, which I humbly and
earnestly again and again intreat you may, being persuaded
that no consideration or solicitation can be powerful enough
to hinder the effects of the generous motions and inclin-
ations which virtue and honour will inspire you for supporting and preserving your near cousin, so honourable and
noble a family and a person of so great merit and so
greatly and deservedly beloved, and after all it may seem
needless to add so inconsiderable a thing, that he is so
very dear to me, and I will be ready so long as I live upon

all occasions to express my grateful acknowledgments of your Lordship's kindness and favour to him which will oblige one so long as I live to be certainly sincerely and with great esteem, my Lord, your Lordship's most faithful and humble servant,

(Signed)   " H. C. of Calder."

" To my Lord Elcho."

NOTES ON AULDEARN, MOY, AND CULLODEN.

By DAVID CAMERON, DAVIOT.

THE records of many a noble and brave action are lost and forgotten ; but tradition occasionally shows us a few flitting glimpses of old heroes who stand out in bold relief in our own time, especially when, in the first place, the records were "bequeathed by bleeding sire to son," and faithfully transmitted from one generation to another, as long as the old martial spirit survived. But the old associations and the old familiar faces pass away ; and it is no longer our privilege to grasp the hands of the old friends, who, in their turn, had grasped the hands of the older friends, who fought and bled for Prince Charles. At the battle of Auldearn, fought on the 4th day of May, 1645, the royal army, commanded by the Marquis of Montrose, was greatly outnumbered by the army of the Convention of Estates, under General Sir John Urray. Accordingly, Montrose posted his right wing within the shelter of some sheep-pens. The right consisted of 400 Scots—Irish musketeers from Antrim—and a small body of Highlanders, all under the command of Sir Alexander Macdonell, better known as Coll Kittoch or the "Left-handed," which was really his father's name, not his own. He had strict orders to hold this strong position, and defend the Royal Standard, which was placed there to draw the main attack of the enemy. The centre consisted of the artillery and a few picked men, screened by the village of Auldearn. The left wing was posted on the west side of the village, where Montrose himself commanded the infantry, and Lord Lewis Gordon the cavalry. Coll Kittoch repulsed the first attack, but he rashly ventured into the open field, where his small

12

force was nearly surrounded by the enemy's cavalry and
infantry. Montrose got notice of this state of matters, but
he kept it secret, and pressed on with the left wing until the
enemy gave way. Reinforcements were then promptly sent
to Coll Kittoch, who, mainly by his personal intrepidity,
had now secured the retreat of his division into the enclosures, from whence he sallied forth again, and the enemy
was quickly routed with the loss of 2000 men. Montrose
lost only 24 gentlemen and a few of the Antrim men.

A redoubtable swordsman, the smith, Robertson Gow,
Macdhonachie), from Struan, in Athole, greatly distinguished himself. He was in the right wing and among the
foremost in the first onset, where it appears his party
attempted to capture some provision carts. The smith
appropriated a small frying-pan, and stowed it inside his
broad, blue bonnet, which he then "scrogged" or pulled
down over his brow. He dived again into the contents of
the cart—and here a curious incident is said to have
occurred. As he was lifting out a few loaves, an English
dragoon rode up behind him, and dealt him a heavy blow
on the head with his sword. But, instead of cleaving the
Highlander's skull, as he intended, the sword recoiled harm-
lessly from the stroke, much to the astonishment of the
trooper, who exclaimed, "Scotie, your *hard* bonnet has
saved your head!" While wearing this queer but useful
head-piece, the smith, along with Coll Kittoch, fought like
lions on the retreat to the enclosures. That evening, as
Robertson was cooking his supper, some of the Antrim
men tried to get possession of his frying-pan; and the row
that followed brought Coll Kittoch upon the scene. "I
think I should have been allowed to prepare my supper in
peace after what I have done to-day," said Vulcan. "How
many men have you killed?" asked Coll Kittoch. "Nine-
teen," said Vulcan. "By Mary! I have killed only
twenty-one myself. You deserve to have the frying-pan,"
said Coll Kittoch, as he gazed in astonishment upon the
brave Vulcan, and asked him, "Who are *you*?" "I am only
a tradesman (fear-ceaird) from Athole," was the unassum-

ing reply. " I wish," said Coll Kittoch, " that every man of
mine was a ' fear-ceaird,' like you."

Robertson thus proved himself to be a worthy repre-
sentative of that remarkable class of men, the Highland
armourers, who made excellent swords, battleaxes, and
other weapons, of the native iron, smelted in the numerous
Highland bloomeries, forged with peat-charcoal, and finely
tempered and handsomely finished.

There was a tradition in Ardnamurchan that Coll Kittoch
once consulted " a very wise old woman" concerning his
destiny. She told him, " You shall always be victorious
until you reach Moulin-coignagō." " Where is that place ?"
he asked her ; but she told him no more. So Coll Kittoch
went his own way ; and he always asked the name of every
place he reached. He joined Montrose ; and after sharing
in several bloody victories, he deserted the Royal standard.
He thus helped to ruin the Royal cause ; and he followed
his own ruthless course through blood and devastation,
until at last he reached Cantire, where, in reply to his
usual question, he got the answer which he dreaded most :
" This is Mounlin-coignagō. The Campbells are coming."
The blood of the helpless and innocent was terribly
avenged.

One day towards the end of July, in the year 1745, as
David Stewart of Kynachan (in Athole), and his men were
making the hay, they observed a man hurrying towards
them with a letter, which he handed to the master. When
Kynachan glanced over the letter, he threw down the hay-
fork, raised his bonnet, and joyfully communicated the
news to his men. " The Prince has landed in Moidart, and
this hand of mine shall never lift either hay-fork or scythe
until I place him on the Throne." This resolute veteran
had formerly distinguished himself in his defence of
Leith in the year 1715. Now, he and his men went forth
to follow Prince Charles, leaving the hay ungathered, and
the garden wall unfinished, as it remains to this day — a sad
memorial shewing that the builders never returned.

Old Mrs Robertson, who lived at Blair-Athole, used long ago to talk a good deal to the writer about Prince Charles. She said :—" My mother remembered very well when Prince Charles and the Highlanders were here (at Blair). She was then a girl of eighteen years of age, and lived with her parents in Glenfin Castle. One day some of the Prince's men visited the glen, and took away the cattle, and our people's cow among the rest. They drove the cattle to this side (N.W.) of Tulloch Hill, near their camp, which was over yonder (said Mrs Robertson, pointing with her staff to the small plateau between Craig Ower and Tulloch Hill). But my mother was very sorry about losing the cow ; so she followed the Highlanders until she saw from the top of the hill where they put the cattle. So, when the evening was getting dark, she went round by this side (north) of the camp, until she came to yonder dyke. Then she called out to the cow, and the cow came running up to her. So my mother knocked down the dyke, and the cow came through the breach, and both trotted home together."

When Lord Loudon, the Commander of the Royal army, then stationed at Inverness, received information from his spies as to the near approach of Prince Charles and his army, he called his officers together, and they planned a night attack, and resolved, if possible, to capture the Prince, who was then at Moyhall ; and the advance guard of his army was encamped at Moybeg ; but it was thought that they did not keep a sufficient guard, as they had newly arrived from the south, and were much fatigued. On the 16th of March, sentries were, accordingly, placed all round the town of Inverness to prohibit any one from leaving ; and, at eight o'clock that evening, Lord Loudon, with a force of 1500 men of the Macleods, some northern clans, and a few regulars, started for Moy ; but not so secretly as they thought, for, at the same time, a lady, who knew the whole scheme, bribed a dragoon to take up a small boy, named Lachlan Mackintosh. He placed the boy behind him, concealed him under his cloak, and let him down outside the sentries. The boy was afraid of being captured, so he went off the road till he got well in advance. He reached Moy in good time. Also a shepherd from Daviot brought to Moy the news of the near approach of the Royal army. The Macleods were in front as they threaded the pass of Moy, called "Starsnach-nan-Gael," or the "Threshold of the Highlands." When they emerged from the pass they lost their way in the dark, and came upon a number of peat-stacks, which they mistook for men, and commenced to fire. Several of those in front, including the piper, were shot by their own men in the rear. Now that the alarm was given, Lord Loudon had to beat a very hasty retreat, which soon became a confused rout.

Other accounts say that Lady Anne Mackintosh received that evening two letters from Inverness, making her aware of Lord Loudon's intentions—one from Fraser of Gortuleg, and the other from her mother ; and that several officers in a tavern in Inverness were overheard by the landlady's daughter discussing the project. She was a young girl of thirteen or fourteen years of age. It is said that she escaped, and ran barefooted to Moy, and told all to Lady Mackintosh, who had employed Donald Fraser, the smith, and six or seven men, to watch the road. Fraser and his men came in contact with the advance guard of the Macleods behind the peat stacks, and raised the alarm. Early next morning, the Prince assembled the greater part of his army, and advanced upon Inverness. Lord Loudon retreated by Kessock Ferry, and took all the boats to the north side. He was finally compelled to retreat to Sutherlandshire. The Mackintosh was then a captain in Lord Loudon's Regiment. He was taken prisoner, and the Prince gave him in charge of his wife, Lady Anne, saying, "That he could not be in better security, or more honourably treated."

The best authorities on this subject are, undoubtedly, Sir Æneas Mackintosh of Mackintosh and Robert Chambers.

Lady Anne Mackintosh was erroneously represented by the English at this time as a powerful amazon, clad in male attire, who rode at the head of her regiment at the Battle of Culloden. Sir Walter Scott is, likewise, mistaken in his History, where he gives an almost similar account of Lady Anne. Sir Æneas Mackintosh, in his valuable Notes written about 1774, and recently printed for The Mackintosh, says that Lady Mackintosh was, at that time (1746), a small, thin lady, twenty years of age, and newly married to Æneas, the (22nd) Chief of Clan Chattan. She never saw the clansmen but once at Moy. She had, however, a very winsome address, and so she persuaded 700 of the Confederacy of Clan Chattan to join the Prince. Their Colonel was Alexander Macgillivray of Dunmaglass. In 1746, they were among the other clans that assembled at Perth, met the Prince at Stirling, and fought at the Battle of Falkirk with their usual intrepidity. Here Dunmaglass had several bullets shot through his plaid. General David Stewart of Garth says, in his Sketches, that " Lady Mackintosh was the daughter of Farquharson of Invercauld ; and of all the fine ladies few were more accomplished, more beautiful, or more enthusiastic."

The piper who fell at the rout of Moy was the celebrated Donald Ban Macrimmen, from Dunvegan, the composer of the famous lament that bears his name (Caraid nan Gaidheal, pp. 380-1). When Macleod of Dunvegan went forth at the head of his clan to join the Royal army at Inverness, the most of the Macleods, if they got their own choice, would have gone to fight for Prince Charles ; and this was the case, particularly, with Macrimmen. In composing the lament " Cha till mi Tuilleadh," he had a strong presentiment that he would never return. There was a great lamentation among the women and children at Dunvegan when the Macleods, with Macrimmen at their head playing this mournful tune, moved down to the shore to embark. Macrimmen was to be married, and he was thus compelled to leave his intended wife at Dunvegan. She was fully convinced that she would see him no more ; and so she composed that beautiful and appropriate song, of which the writer ventures herewith to give a translation :—

MACRIMMEN'S LAMENT.

The mist o'er the Coolin was sweeping,
The Banshee did eerily mourn ;
A maid in Dunvegan is weeping
For him who will never return.
    Macrimmen will never return—
    Departed forever and aye,
    In peace he will never return
    Or war till the Gathering Day.

The breezes so faintly are sighing,
The streamlets so languidly mourn ;
The birds in the grove are replying,
" Macrimmen will never return."
    Macrimmen will never return.

The ocean behind thee is wailing,
The boat would yet wilfully stay,
And plaintively murmur in sailing,
" Macrimmen's departing for aye."
    Macrimmen will never return.

The pibroch no longer is pealing
At eve on the echoing shore ;
The youth of the castle and sheiling
Are charmed by thy music no more.
    Macrimmen will never return—
    Departed for ever and aye,
    In peace he will never return
    Or war till the Gathering Day.

At the battle of Culloden, on the 16th of April, 1746, the Prince's regiments in the front line, from right to left, were— Athole, Cameron, Appin, Fraser, Mackintosh or Clan Chattan, Maclauchlan and Maclean, John Roy Stewart, Clan Ranald, Keppoch, Glengarry. In the second line, from right to left, were—Lord Ogilvie, Lord Lewis Gordon, Glenbucket, Duke of Perth, the Irish and the French. Four cannons were at each flank, and also four in the centre. Lord George Murray commanded the right wing, Lord John Drummond the left, and General Stapleton the second line. The Prince stood in the rear with a small body of cavalry. Tht total number was aboue 5000 men.

In the royal army the regiments were disposed in three lines ; in the first, from left to right, were—Burrel (the 4th), Munro (37th), Scots Fusileers (21st), Price (14th), Cholmondley (34th), Scots Royals (1st) ; in the second line, in the same order—Wolfe (8th), Sempill (25th), Bligh (20th), Ligonier (48th), Fleming (35th) ; in the third line—Blakeney (27th), Batterean (13th), Howard (3rd) ; on the left were Kerr's Dragoons (11th) ; and in the rear were Cobham's Dragoons (10th) and the Campbells In the first line, two cannons (6-pounders) were placed between every two regiments. The Earl of Albemarle commanded the first line, General Huske the second, Brigadier Mordaunt the third, and Colonel Belford the artillery. The total number was fully 9000 men.

The Commander-in-Chief, the Duke of Cumberland, made the most careful preparations. The different positions of the two armies, before the battle, have never been very precisely ascertained ; but the main distance between them was about 500 yards—not in parallel lines, for the opposing right and left wings were nearer each other. The Highlanders faced to the east, or nearly so, with the disadvantage of the sleet, and also the smoke from the English lines, blowing in their faces. The Clans were exposed for half-an-hour (about 1—1.30) to a very destructive artillery fire ; so that the death of so many of their friends rendered them furious and impatient for the onset. The general order to charge was never delivered, as the Prince's aide-de-camp, a young man, named Maclauchlan, was killed by a cannon ball as he started with the order ; and so the attack made by the right and centre was not simultaneous. The Macdonalds, on the left wing, refused to advance, because they were not allowed their usual precedence of fighting on the right wing. They, therefore, retired to the second line.

The Mackintoshes or Confederacy of Clan Chattan, 700 strong, struck the first blow at this battle. They were led by their Colonel (Macgillivray of Dunmaglass). "Come, my lads,' he said in Gaelic, 'fall in, your faces to Fortrose and your backs to the Green of Muirtown—load your fire-

locks—present—now take good aim—fire." One of the
corps, named John Grant, Aviemore, used to tell that the
first thing he saw of the enemy was the long line of white
gaiters belonging to an English regiment, which was
suddenly revealed, when about twenty yards from him, by
a blast of wind which blew aside the smoke (Chamber's
History). In spite of the English musketry and grape-
shot poured upon them like a hailstorm, they cut their way
sword in hand right through Burrel's and Munroe's
regiments of the first English line, and with unabated fury
charged Sempill's regiment in the second line. This regiment was drawn up three men deep, with the front rank
kneeling. When the fugitives from Burrel's and Munroe's
regiments escaped to the rear, Sempill's battalion poured
in their fire on the Mackintoshes when they were almost at
the bayonet points. Still a few pressed on, but failed to
break through this steady corps (Scott's History). About
400 of the Mackintoshes fell in this dreadful charge; and
they lost all their officers except three, and one of these
was severely wounded. Their Colonel (Dunmaglass) was
shot through the heart, and fell in the centre of Burrel's
regiment (Notes by Sir Æneas Mackintosh). Their
Major (John More Macgillivray) cut his way all alone
through the centre of Sempill's regiment in the second line,
where he was surrounded ; he killed a dozen men with his
broadsword ere he was cut down by the English halberts
(Chamber's History). The standard bearer was shot dead,
but a comrade seized the colours, tore them off the pole,
wrapped them round his breast, and carried them safely
from the field (Notes by Sir Æ. M.) In the retreat one
of their sergeants, a gigantic young Highlander named
Gillies Macbean, from Faillie, was in the rear and wounded.
He was attacked by the dragoons, but he set his back
against a wall, and fought them single-handed with his
broadsword and target. Some of the officers tried in vain
to draw off their men, as they wished to save the brave
fellow. It is said that, ere he fell, 13 of his enemies lay
dead around him.

The other clans in the centre and right wing were not slow in following the example of the Mackintoshes. They also cut their way through the first English line, and joined in the attack upon Sempill's and Bligh's regiments in the second line, but they also suffered severely from the fire of the musketry and grape shot, and also from the cross-fire of Wolfe's regiment that was drawn across the flank of the right wing. The English cavalry attempted to get round both flanks, but they were kept in check by the fire of the second line, which was now joined by the Macdonalds. Lord Elcho urged the Prince to place himself at the head of this body and charge the enemy ; but General Sullivan seized the Prince's bridle and urged him to quit the field. Sir Thomas Sheridan and other favourites pressed round him and bore him off (Scott's Hist.). Alexander Macdonald of Keppoch was badly wounded as he advanced almost alone. He urged his nephew to save himself ; and still he pressed on until he was shot dead. The Camerons lost nearly 300 men. Donald Cameron, younger of Lochiel, their Colonel, was severely wounded in both legs by the grape shot, and was carried by two of his kinsmen to the south side of the river Nairn. The Colonel of the Frasers, Charles Fraser, younger of Inverallochy, lay wounded on the field, and was shot by Cumberland's orders, executed by a private soldier, after several officers had declined to do it, including Major Wolfe, who said to the Duke that he would rather resign his commission than become an executioner. In the Appin regiment 17 officers and gentlemen were killed, and 10 were wounded. Their Colonel, Charles Stewart of Ardshiel, escaped unhurt. The Chief of Maclauchlan, Colonel of the regiment of Maclauchlan and Maclean, was shot dead in the onset. Then Maclean of Drumnin assumed the command of the regiment ; and, as he was retreating with the survivors, he saw two of his sons severely wounded by his side ; and he heard that a third was killed. " It shall not be for nought," he said, as he rushed back and attacked two dragoons, and killed one and wounded the other. He was himself killed by other three

who came up (Chambers' History). The Atholemen lost
nearly as many men as the Mackintoshes, being on the
extreme right, and fully exposed to the cross-fire of Wolfe's
regiment, as well as to the musketry and grape shot in
front. They were led by their Colonel, Lord George
Murray, a veteran of great experience, and a general of the
highest ability. Lord George was present at Sheriffmuir in
1715, and at Glenshiel in 1719. But he was no favourite
with the Prince, because he always stated his opinions
rather plainly ; and the Irish officers, who had nothing to
lose, generally advised something different. He escaped
from the field unhurt. David Stewart of Kynachan was
shot dead among the foremost. A clansman, who fell
severely wounded beside him, thus records his experience of
that terrible day to his grand-nephew, who communicated
the same to the writer :—" I fell severely wounded in the
charge. I lay all day upon the field. I became conscious
towards the evening. A wounded Englishman (Sassenach)
was stretched beside me. As the evening darkened, I saw
at some distance the form of an old woman moving
stealthily among the dead and wounded that thickly
strewed the field. I saw her over and over again lifting a
large stone, and throwing it at the heads of the wounded,
whom she thus killed and robbed. I said to my wounded
companion, 'See what yonder old woman is doing ! She
will come here soon and do the same to us both.' He
looked at her and saw her atrocious conduct. For a while
we did not know what to do. I implored him to try to
shoot her. He said that his musket was unloaded, and
asked me if I had a charge in mine. I said that I thought
it was loaded when I fell. He asked me to hand the
musket over to him, which I did. He slowly raised himself
on one knee, took aim, and fired, and down she fell ! I
then tried to creep away from the field, and came to a
ditch which I could not cross in my weak condition. A
Highlander in King George's army stood on guard on the
other side of the ditch. I begged of him to help me over,
but he turned away, saying, 'God help you all ! for every

wounded man of you will be shot to-morrow morning.' He turned back, however, stretched his hand across to me, and with his face half-turned another way, he pulled me over the ditch. I made my way towards the hills (of Strathdearn ?), and when the night was well advanced, I came to a malt kiln, entered it, and lay down upon the warm grain. But the warmth of the kiln caused my wounds to bleed anew. So I got up and walked on a little further, until I reached a cottage, which I entered. The only inmate was an old woman, who received me very kindly, helped me to dress my wounds, and afterwards furnished me with food and a bed. I was greatly refreshed next day, and I continued my journey homewards."

While the second line of the Prince's army, under General Stapleton, left the field with pipes playing and banners flying, and went to Inverness, where they surrendered upon honourable terms, the Prince, with about 1200 of the survivors of Clan Chattan, the Athole men, the Camerons, and the Macdonalds, took the Strathnairn road, and crossed the River Nairn below Ballinluig of Faillie. After a brief halt and consultation on the plain, they broke up; the Mackintoshes and the Athole men turned to the left, and took the road to Moy; the Camerons and the Macdonalds to the right, on the road to Lochaber. The Prince, with a few cavalry and intimate friends, turned westwards, and commenced his wanderings. At the same time, the English dragoons were dogging their footsteps in order to kill the wounded and the stragglers.

Two brothers lived with their parents at Ballinluig; one brother went to Culloden, but the other one was kept at home, because he was considered to be " half-witted," and his friends were afraid that his conduct might not be quite heroic. Towards evening the other one was chased on the moor by the English troopers. He came bounding down to his father's house just as a trooper appeared on the ridge. The two brothers met at the end of the house, and the half-witted one exclaimed sarcastically : " Hallo ! has the hero returned ? Give me your musket—run in and get a piece (of bread) from your mother—now go and hide yourself in the broom!" So the "half-witted one" stood and fought the trooper, shot him dead, loaded again, and shot the horse. The horse and his rider were buried together below the old garden, and the grave is still locally known.

A young lad named Shaw, belonging to the Mackintosh Regiment, retreating from Culloden, entered his father's house at Altlugie, but was closely pursued by a dragoon, who followed him into the house and shot him. Next day the same dragoon reached this farm-house, and entered it with his sword drawn. The murdered lad's sister was baking bread, and the dragoon moved towards her, and threatened her with his sword. She instantly threw her apron over the naked sword, sprang on the dragoon, wrenched his weapon out of his hand, and with it stabbed him to the heart, saying, "Take that for killing my brother yesterday!" One of her friends shot the trooper's horse in order to conceal the matter more effectually; so the man and his horse were buried at once on the green at the east-end of the house. On the morning of the battle, a certain gentleman living in Strathdearn, sent two boys with a letter down to a gentleman near Culloden. On their way down through Strathnairn they were much surprised to meet detached parties, and also individual soldiers, of the Prince's army in full retreat up the Strath, for it was not expected that the battle would be fought so soon, and, least of all, that it would end in this disastrous manner to the Highlanders. The two boys, however, proceeded on their way, and delivered the letter. They afterwards proposed to go to the field of battle. They were not long on the battle-field when they were espied by the English dragoons, two of whom galloped towards them, but the boys fled to the hills, followed by the two troopers. One of the boys fell as his foot was tripped by the heather, and he received a severe cut in the leg from the trooper's sword. He was not, however, further molested, and his friends afterwards came and took him home. Meanwhile,

the other boy, who was swifter, was more fortunate.   He
made straight for a peat moss, and dodged about, and very
soon the trooper's horse sank in the moss.   The boy now
joined other retreating friends, and ere he crossed the ridge
he looked back and saw his pursuer vainly trying to pull
his horse out of the moss.

The old people used to point out what they regarded
as bullet-marks on the rock at the mouth of the cave below
Clach-na-Houllie (the treasure-trove stone), on the right
bank of the Nairn at Daltullich   It is said that this
cave afforded shelter to several of the clansmen, and that
the English fired upon them from the opposite side of the
river.   There are two mounds in the middle of Daviot
Wood, near a ruined bothy, which are still regarded as the
graves of two Highlanders who fell on the retreat from
Culloden.   About a mile further up the valley, as several
workmen were engaged on the 14th June, 1882, in cutting
a new road they came upon several skeletons.   On the
shoulder of one of the skeletons was found a rude copper
plaid-brooch, which was seen by the writer.   A few threads
of coarse woollen cloth were wound round the root of the
brooch-pin.   This interesting relic, preserved in Moyhal,
may be fairly regarded as a sad memento of this fatal day

The Ettrick Shepherd's song on the Stewarts of Appin
is quite applicable to all the clans who fought at Culloden :—

"And ne'er for the crown of the Stuarts was fought
One battle on vale, or on mountain deer-trodden,
But dearly to Appin the glory was bought,
And dearest of all on the field of Culloden !
Clan Chattan is broken, the Seaforth bends low,
The sun of Clan Ranald is sinking in labour ;
Glencoe and Clan Donnachie, where are they now ?
And where is bold Keppoch, the lord of Lochaber ?
All gone with the house they supported !—laid low,
While dogs of the south their bold life-blood were
     lapping,
Trod down by a proud and a merciless foe—
The brave are all gone with the Stuarts of Appin.
Their glory is o'er, for their star is no more,
And the green grass waves over the heroes of Appin !"

NOTES.

Mr Magnus Maclean, M.A., well known to our readers for his papers on the "Skye Bards," has published in the first number of the Proceedings of the Clan Maclean Society a concise account of the "Maclean Bards," with choice specimens of their poetry, both English and Gaelic.

Mr Alex. Mackenzie, of the *Scottish Highlander*, has just published a sumptuous "Guide to Inverness," extending to some one hundred and twenty pages, with numerous and excellently executed illustrations. The historical portion of the work is concise and more accurate than any account we have hitherto seen of the town, while the descriptive part is happy both in the choice of its subjects and its language. Numerous excursions are detailed to various places of interest within a radius of two dozen miles.

Professor Zimmer, of Greifswald, is still unremittingly pursuing his Celtic Researches. In the last number of the Comparative Philology *Zeitschrift*, he has an article upon old Irish Charms of the Viking Period. Professor Zimmer wishes to prove that Irish charms as well as Irish Fenian heroes belong to the Norse. But he has adduced a somewhat obscure word—viz., *héle*, an incantation, which throws light on an obscurely worded Gaelic charm, published in the third volume of the *Highland Monthly* (p. 224).

This charm, known as "Eòlas nan Sul," was copied from *Cuairtear Nan Gleann*, of 1842, and ran as follows :—

" Obaidh nan geur shùl
An obaidh 's feàrr fo 'n ghrein
Obaidh Dhé, an uile mhòir.
Féile Mhairi, féile Dhé,
Féile gach sagairt 's gach cléir,
Feile Mhichael nam feart,
'Chàirich anns a' ghréin a neart."

The translation of *féile* hitherto offered has been "generosity;" but we see from Professor Zimmer's researches that this must be changed to "charm" or "incantation." The translation will run thus:—" Incantation for sore-smarting eyes, the best incantation 'neath the sun, the incantation of God All-great; charm of Mary, charm of God, charm of each priest and cleric, charm of Michael the doughty, who bestowed on the sun its strength."

WHILE on the subject of " Charms," we may add two more unpublished ones, found among Dr Cameron's papers. They are both entitled " Seun," but no word of explanation is vouchsafed. The first runs thus :—

> " Diombuan 'ga bhuain,
> Is buan 'ga chaitheamh,
> *As* dà-s' 's *ann* duinne."

That is to say : " Short be its reaping and long its consuming; *out* (of the ground) with it, but let us be *in it* (live)." This charm, doubtless, refers to corn reaping, or some such process. The other charm is as follows :—

> " Tiobairt mhòr an druim an tighe,
> Salann 's sùidh 's tigh so ;
> An sgeul thug thu stigh air barr do theang'   .
> Gu'm b'anr bheireadh tu mach air barr d'earbuill e !"

The translation is : " A large well (?) in the midst of this house ; salt and soot be in this house ; the tale thou bringest in on the tip of thy tongue, mayst thou take it out on the tip of thy tail !" It is a somewhat enigmatic charm.

A HIGHLAND MEMORY:

Personal Reminiscences of the North, both grave and gay.

BY AN OLD COLONIAL.

With *FORTY-FIVE ORIGINAL DRAWINGS* and *SKETCHES* by the Author.

(Specimen Illustration)

IN drawing public attention to this work, the Publishers feel assured that they will earn the thanks of all who appreciate true and delicate humour, frank and generous sentiment, and vivid and accurate portrayal of Scottish character; and they are confident that the book needs only to be known to obtain an extensive and ever-widening circle of admirers and readers. It is elegantly printed, and profusely adorned with vigorous illustrations, full of character and incident, and it is published at a popular price, so as to place it within the reach of all!

PRICE ONE SHILLING

To be had of all Newsagents and Bookstalls, or Post Free, 1s 2d

"NORTHERN CHRONICLE" OFFICE, INVERNESS

LONDON: SIMPKIN, MARSHALL, HAMILTON, KENT & CO., LTD

[OVER

Press Notices.

"A capital book for holiday reading. It is light enough to be amusing, is minute enough to be accepted as a broadly-drawn sketch of what actually happens at holiday times in out of the way corners of the West Highlands, and has enough of connected romance in it to maintain the interest of the reader."—*Glasgow Herald.*

"It is a quiet, slowly going, yet always comically satirical account of the everyday life of a remote place in the Western Highlands. The abundance of fun in the book, and its sprinkling of sentiment, are quite enough to palliate any departure from nature in depicting Highland character."—*Scotsman.*

"The author is a Scotchman, and not only can appreciate humour in others, but is somewhat of a humourist himself."—*Manchester Examiner.*

Should be found in every Scottish household."—*Argus.*

"To the gay, its perusal will enhance the pleasures of a holiday, or compensate for the want of one; and to the grave, will open up views of life, and lines of thought, which they may ponder with advantage."--*The Cateran.*

The Highland Monthly.

VOL. V.

A Magazine which is intended to be a Centre
of Literary Brotherhood for Scoto-Celtic
People both at Home and Abroad.

LIST OF CONTRIBUTORS.

*The following, among others, are to be
Contributors :—*

Lord ARCHIBALD CAMPBELL, Author of "Records
of Argyll."

Sir HENRY COCKBURN MACANDREW, Provost of
Inverness

CHAS. FRASER-MACKINTOSH, Esq., M.P., Author
of "Antiquarian Notes," "Dunachton Past and
Present," "Invernessiana," &c.

Rev. HUGH MACMILLAN, LL.D., D.D., Author of
"Bible Teachings in Nature," "Foot-Notes
from the Page of Nature," &c.

Rev. JAMES CAMERON LEES, D.D., Minister of
St Giles, Edinburgh, Dean of the Thistle and
Chapel Royal.

Rev. Dr MASSON, Author of "Vestigia Celtica."

Rev. JAMES ROBERTSON, D.D., Superintendent of
Presbyterian Missions, Manitoba and N.W.T.

JOSEPH ANDERSON, Esq., LL.D., Keeper of the
Museum of Antiquities, Royal Institution, Edinburgh.

A. C. CAMERON, LL.D., Fettercairn.

JOHN MACKINTOSH, Esq., LL.D., Author of the
"History of Civilization in Scotland."

ANDREW J. SYMINGTON, Esq., Glasgow, Editor of
"Wordsworth."

P. J. ANDERSON, Esq., Secretary of the New
Spalding Club, Aberdeen.

Rev. JOHN MACLEAN of Grandtully, Author of
"Breadalbane Place Names."

JAMES CRABB WATT, Esq., Edinburgh, F.S.A.
Scot., Author and Editor of Popular Bio-
graphies.

Rev. JOHN CAMPBELL, Minister of Tiree.

Rev. J. M. MACGREGOR, Minister of Farr, Sutherland.

Rev. JOHN M'RURY, Minister of Snizort, Skye.

Rev. J. SINCLAIR, Minister of Rannoch.

"M. O. W.," Russia.

CHARLES INNES, Esq., Sheriff-Clerk of Ross-shire.

GEORGE MALCOLM, Esq., Invergarry.

ALEX. MACPHERSON, Esq., Solicitor, Kingussie.

WM. MACKAY, Esq., Solicitor, Inverness.

KENNETH MACDONALD, Esq., Town-Clerk of
Inverness.

JOHN CAMPBELL, Esq., Ledaig, Author of Gaelic
Poems.

Rev. T. SINTON, Minister of Dores.

T. COCKBURN, Esq., M.A., Royal Academy Inverness

CHRISTOPHER T. MICHIE, Esq., Cullen, Author of
"The Practice of Forestry" "The Larch" &c.